THE JUDGE TURNED TOWARD HIM...

"I hereby order the U.S. marshal to lead you to the gallows at ten of the clock tomorrow morning. There, the hangman will put a knotted noose around your neck and then pull the trapdoor lever, thereby dropping your filthy, raping, murdering, stealing carcass ten feet, where you will either break your neck or swing in the breeze. You will hang there as the townsfolk look at your miserable corpse, and then your worthless body will be cut down, placed in a crude pine box, and buried six feet underground in a potter's field, where the worms and maggots can have free rein over what is left of your mortal body..."

Other Exciting Westerns in Avon Books'
REMINGTON Series

(#1) WEST OF THE PECOS

Coming Soon

(#3) SHOWDOWN AT COMANCHE BUTTE

Avon Books are available at special quantity discounts for bulk purchases for sales promotions, premiums, fund raising or educational use. Special books, or book excerpts, can also be created to fit specific needs.

For details write or telephone the office of the Director of Special Markets, Avon Books, Dept. FP, 105 Madison Avenue, New York, New York 10016.

REMINGTON #2

GOOD DAY FOR A HANGIN'

JAMES CALDER BOONE

AVON
PUBLISHERS OF BARD, CAMELOT, DISCUS AND FLARE BOOKS

REMINGTON #2: GOOD DAY FOR A HANGIN' is an original publication of Avon Books. This work has never before appeared in book form.

AVON BOOKS
A division of
The Hearst Corporation
105 Madison Avenue
New York, New York 10016

Copyright © 1987 by James Calder Boone
Published by arrangement with the author
Produced in cooperation with Taneycomo Productions, Inc., Branson, Missouri
Library of Congress Catalog Card Number: 87-91117
ISBN: 0-380-75266-2

All rights reserved, which includes the right to reproduce this book or portions thereof in any form whatsoever except as provided by the U.S. Copyright Law. For information address Taneycomo Productions, Inc., P.O. Box 1069, Branson, Missouri 65616.

First Avon Printing: June 1987

AVON TRADEMARK REG. U.S. PAT. OFF. AND IN OTHER COUNTRIES, MARCA REGISTRADA, HECHO EN U.S.A.

Printed in the U.S.A.

K-R   10   9   8   7   6   5   4   3   2   1

Prologue

The man had already tried to escape twice. And twice Chief Territorial Marshal Ned Remington had caught him, put him in irons. He wasn't about to let the son of a bitch run away again. He would shoot him first, and not twitch a muscle when he did it. Leroy Switcher was a mean bastard, the scum of the earth. Cocky, too, and Ned hated that in a man, especially in a criminal like Switcher.

The warrant Remington carried in his coat pocket had taken him to the Nations, into Creek and Choctaw lands, where Switcher was hiding from the law and Judge Samuel Parkhurst Barnstall's Western District Circuit Court of Missouri. Switcher had been charged with murder, robbery, and rape. There were two surviving eyewitnesses sitting in a hotel in Galena, Missouri, waiting to testify against Switcher. Ned didn't want to disappoint any of them, so he kept hard, cold eyes on

Switcher as the man rode ahead of the marshal, his wrists handcuffed.

"Damn, Remington, I gotta have a smoke," said Switcher, a lanky, rawboned man in his late twenties. His face was ferret-thin, with deep wrinkles around the mouth, next to his slender, sharp-pointed nose. He wore three days of stubble on his chin, which gave him the appearance of having dipped it in soot. He wore gray duck trousers, a patched linsey-woolsey shirt open at the throat, boots that had lost their tan shine and were cracking from the dryness. His dark brown eyes glittered in deep sockets and restlessly searched the land around him like an animal's. His battered felt hat shaded his forehead as the morning sun climbed above the trees. They had been riding since dawn, without a stop, after spending the night in Siloam Springs, just inside the Arkansas border.

"When I say so, Switcher," said Remington softly. His voice at that level sounded like an echo in a cave; his words were hollow, rumbling like far-off thunder.

"Feel like I'm sittin' on a ax blade," said Switcher. "Damn saddle's 'bout to cut both cheeks off."

Remington didn't reply, and Switcher cackled at his own humor. That was the cockiness in him, thought Ned. Switcher was brash and fancied himself irresistible to the ladies. When they refused his attentions, he was apt to lash out violently at their stupidity. It had gotten him in trouble more than once. But the last time he had gone too far, and had beaten the woman senseless in front of witnesses. Then he had raped her and strangled her during the act. She had died, and Switcher had taken her money and valuables and then run off to the Nations with two of his cronies.

Remington had intended to halt this side of Eureka Springs, but not until they reached the hills and hollows just south of town. They were near the battlefield now, Elkhorn Tavern, the rebs called it. The Union called it Pea Ridge. It was more open here, and ever since leaving Tahlequah Switcher had bragged about never going back over the Missouri border. The two men who had run off with him had lit a shuck when Remington captured Switcher. But once, two days ago, Ned had crossed the fresh tracks of two shod horses, and yesterday he had seen a rider slip over a distant hill less than a thousand yards ahead of them.

Maybe neither incident meant anything, but Leroy Switcher had been restless as a long-tailed cat in a room full of rocking chairs ever since they had left the Choctaw Nation. And no sign of Leroy's friends since Ned had put Switcher in irons. Not close up, anyway.

Remington transferred his reins from his right hand to his left. His right hand came to rest on the butt of his pistol, a .44-caliber converted Remington New Model Army. Two more pistols hung from his saddlehorn: a Smith & Wesson .38, nickled, which he sometimes wore in a shoulder holster, and a Colt .44 with an eight-inch barrel. His rifle, a '73 Winchester in .44-40 caliber, jutted from its leather boot within easy reach.

Some instinct began to prick at Remington's senses like the jabbing spines of a Spanish bayonet. Switcher was doing everything he could to get them to stop and dismount. Why? He was always whining about something, but this time was different. Ned couldn't put his finger on it, but Switcher had something up his sleeve besides his arm.

The land began to drop off, then pitch toward the first hollow after the long ride on the flat. Beyond, the Ozark Mountains, a fiery green, loomed like islands in a sea. Remington looked around one last time.

And that's when he saw it.

His blood froze and something clawed at his innards. It was only a flick of light, a brief shot of sun glinting off the surface of metal, but it was enough.

The flash came from the trees to their left, a thick stand of hickory, pine, oak, surrounded by thickets of sassafras and Osage orange.

"Goddam you, Switcher," Remington said, and he dug spurs into his mount, kicking his horse into motion. The animal lurched ahead. Switcher, startled at the sudden movement, turned, his eyes wide with fear. Remington rode up to him and swung a roundhouse right. His fist caught Switcher behind the ear, sent him toppling.

The outlaw hit the dust, skidding into a heap along the rutted road, as Remington swung over the side of his horse and drew his six-gun.

The riders came out of the trees on fleet horses, their rifles cracking flame and lead. Repeaters, Remington thought, and he waited behind his horse, cocking the hammer back on the forty-four. Dust spouts kicked up all around him, and the marshal suppressed a smile.

"That would be your friends, Switcher," he said evenly.

Switcher looked at the marshal as he would at a madman.

The bushwhackers came on, their horses stretching out, manes flying, as they closed the distance. They shouted rebel yells and leveled their rifles, took aim that never centered. Bullets fired the air, whistled off harmlessly.

"Come on, Leroy!" shouted one of the men. "Get your sweet ass up on that horse."

Remington stepped to his saddle, rested his pistol butt on the seat, and shot the rider in the chest. The wounded man threw his rifle up in the air. It flew end over end and hit the ground before the man did.

The other rider hesitated, started to rein his horse sideways.

Ned cocked his pistol again, took careful aim, and squeezed the two-pound trigger.

The lead ball struck the charging rider in the brisket and tore out a lung before it broke a hole in his back as big as a fist. Blood sprayed from the man's mouth as he left the saddle and hit the ground in a sickening skid.

"Jesus Christ," breathed Switcher, "you killed both of them."

Remington ejected the empty hulls, put two fresh cartridges into his pistol. He walked over to Switcher, picked him up by the collar. He put the pistol barrel up to his prisoner's lips and forced them open. He slid the barrel inside Switcher's mouth.

"And if there was any question that I wouldn't kill them," he said, "I'd have blown your stupid brains to pulp. First."

Switcher swallowed hard. Beads of sweat broke out over his forehead. He began to tremble.

"Christ, Marshal," he said, "I got to go. I got to go real bad."

"Piss your pants, you son of a bitch," said Remington.

His smile made Switcher's face go chalk, and it stayed that way all the way to Galena, Missouri, where Judge Samuel Parkhurst Barnstall was preparing to sit on the bench in Western District Circuit Court.

Chapter One

Fred Loomis wasn't the only barber in Galena, Missouri, but his establishment was the barbershop closest to the courthouse, so when he applied to the court to be the jail barber he got the contract. He knew they had brought in a new prisoner yesterday, so he wasn't surprised when he was summoned to the jail barbershop for a special job.

His customer was Amos Mordecai Cullimore, brought in for murdering an Indian girl in Tahlequah, a small settlement down in the Nations. Fred sharpened his scissors as Cullimore shuffled in with a guard, then settled into the barber chair as comfortably as his leg shackles would allow. Cullimore spoke jovially to the barber.

"Jes' a little off the top, barber, and a nice trim over the ears." The prisoner ran his hand across the top of his head. "I don't get to a barber all that often, so I want you to do a particular nice job."

"You slickin' up for your appointment with the hangman, are you, Cullimore?" the guard asked.

Cullimore laughed. "Don't want to spoil your party none, but that's an appointment I don't reckon to keep."

"What makes you think that?"

"Let's jes' say that I been around a bit, and I know how to play the game." Cullimore leaned back in the chair. "Okay, barber, get to cuttin'."

Samuel Parkhurst Barnstall, a thick-chested, broad-shouldered man with piercing blue eyes and a square chin, stalked through the door of the jail barbershop. He wore a dark suit, slim silk tie, and white shirt. He seemed tall because of his bulk, but he was under six feet. Men who stood in judgment before him would always swear that he was several inches above six feet. When he came into the room he cast a shadow over the barber and the ankle-shackled man sitting in the chair. The scissors clacked like the mandibles of an insect over the shorn edges of his clipped hair. The prisoner looked up at the big man.

Outside, the sounds of hammering could be heard.

"You'd be Amos Mordecai Cullimore," the big man said.

"How'd you know that?"

"I looked at your case records over coffee this morning."

The sound of hammering grew louder.

"What's that infernal racket?" Cullimore asked irritably. "Can't a man even get a haircut in peace?"

"The sound you hear is the building of your scaffold, Cullimore."

Cullimore grunted. "Judge Binder ain't gonna hang me."

"Binder's no longer the judge," the big man said. "I took over his chair."

Cullimore looked up at Barnstall, a flicker of uncertainty in his eyes.

"You the new judge?"

"I am. The name is Samuel Parkhust Barnstall."

"Binder would have let me go free."

"How much did you pay him?"

"A hunnert dollars. Do you the same."

Fred Loomis stepped away from the chair then, finished with Cullimore's hair. The guard stepped up and pulled the prisoner from the chair as the barber shook out the towel.

"You can't buy mercy from my court," said Barnstall.

"Well, I ain't goin' to hang anyways," Cullimore said. He looked into a mirror to check his haircut.

Barnstall's eyebrows arched, like a pair of woolly caterpillars going over a hump.

"Oh? And where did you get that information?"

"I got me witnesses said I didn't go anywheres near that store and kill that woman over to Tahlequah. 'Sides, she were a squaw anyways."

"The witnesses. Are you speaking of the Messrs. Woods and Sisley?"

"Damned right I am," Cullimore said.

Barnstall laughed. "I'm afraid they won't do you much good."

"Why not?"

"I intend to allow them to testify, then instruct the jury to disregard the testimony."

"What? You gonna tell the court not to pay any regard to my witnesses?" Cullimore strained against the guard's grip on his arms.

Judge Barnstall did not back away as the prisoner

got one arm free and reached out for the jurist's throat. The guard grabbed the arm, pinned it back as his face flushed and swelled with the effort.

The judge sat down in the chair vacated by the prisoner, threw his shoulders back, and smiled.

"I am glad you brought those two in, though. Did me a favor, Cullimore. We've been looking for them, too."

"Huh?"

"You'll all three hang together."

Cullimore, enraged, struggled to break free, lunged two feet toward the chair. The guard put a knee in the prisoner's back, snaked an arm around Cullimore's throat. The prisoner gagged, his eyes bulging as if the hatred would boil out of them in a hiss of hot steam.

"You . . . you got to give me a fair trial," gasped Cullimore.

"Oh, it'll be fair."

"In front of a jury."

"Of my peers," said the judge.

"I thought it was *my* peers," Cullimore said.

"You thought wrong. There'll be no murderers or thieves or swine like you sitting in my jury box."

"Hell, Judge, you done got your mind made up."

"That's right, Cullimore," Barnstall said easily.

"What's fair about that?"

"I don't know. Maybe on your way to hell you can ask that Indian woman you killed in cold blood. That is, after your spine snaps like a dry twig, and your face turns purple as you gasp for breath with that hangman's knot behind your ear."

"You son of a bitch. I'll appeal," Cullimore swore.

Judge Barnstall snapped his fingers at the dumbfounded barber, pointed to his hair.

"Just a light trim, Fred," he said softly, as if he didn't even hear Cullimore's words.

"Didn't you hear me, you fuckin' bastard? I said I'd appeal to the Supreme Court. You can't railroad a man to the gallows."

Cullimore struggled, but the guard started backing him toward the door. He was bigger than Cullimore.

"I'll appeal... I'll appeal!" Cullimore gasped.

The judge looked toward Cullimore as if surprised that he was still there. Then, almost as an afterthought, he explained a few things to the enraged prisoner.

"Oh, didn't they tell you, Cullimore? There's no appeal from my court. Not if you committed a crime in the Nations. For your information, I can do any damned thing I want." He paused as the barber threw a fresh towel around his neck. The cloth settled regally on his wide shoulders like a mantle of snowy ermine. "And," the judge continued, "I want to see you hang by your scruffy neck until dead."

"No!" Cullimore said. "No, you can't do this to me, you son of a bitch! I paid Binder a hunnert dollars! I'm being cheated! I'm being cheated!"

Cullimore's voice receded down the hall as the guard took him back to his cell. Judge Samuel Parkhurst Barnstall sighed as Fred began snapping his scissors across the big man's hair.

Judge Barnstall had recently taken over the corrupt court of Lucius Binder under direct authorization of the governor of Missouri, Benjamin Gratz Brown, a Republican elected in November 1870. As the scissors clacked quietly over Barnstall's head, he recalled his meeting with Governor Ben Brown. It seemed like ages ago they had shared a lunch in the governor's office while the governor gave him his commission and his instructions.

"I have the full cooperation of the United States government on this, Sam," the governor said. "You are to implement a force of U.S. territorial marshals with broad powers to cross state lines, work without written warrants, search and seize, do whatever is necessary to bring criminals to justice."

"With no interference?" Barnstall asked.

"With no interference," the governor promised. He buttered a piece of steaming bread and transferred it to his mouth. Just before he took a bite, he spoke again. "The Nations have been a sanctuary for murderers, thieves, and rapists too long. The federal government doesn't want it to go on, and I don't want that kind of sanctuary to exist just across our state line. Do whatever has to be done."

"All right," Barnstall answered.

"Do you have any ideas who you might get to serve as the chief of your marshals?" the governor asked as he chewed a bite of bread.

"Yes," Barnstall said. "I have just the man."

Barnstall didn't elaborate with the governor, but shortly after he left Jefferson City he contacted the one man he knew could do the job. The man was Ned Remington, already serving as a legitimate U.S. marshal. Barnstall had empowered Remington with the authority to deputize as many men as he might need, whenever and wherever he needed them. He made but one stipulation: If any deputy U.S. marshal broke any state or federal laws while in the service of the court, he would be tried and sentenced for any crime or crimes committed while under the court's jurisdiction.

Fred finished with the haircut and Judge Barnstall thanked him, then stepped outside to look toward the gallows. The construction job was nearly completed. All that was left was for him to do his job in the courtroom. That he intended to do.

"All rise!"

There was a scrape of chairs, a rustle of pants, petticoats, and skirts, as the spectators in the courtroom stood. A spittoon rang as one male member of the gallery made a last-second, accurate expectoration of his tobacco quid.

Ned Remington, a tall, strapping man with wide shoulders and a stubble-blue chin, stepped through a door behind the railing and surveyed the gallery. His eyes were gray as iron. He was wearing a converted Remington forty-four low on his hip, easy to reach with his long, lean arms. When he moved, he walked on the balls of his feet like a stalking cougar, or a prizefighter. A United States marshal's star glistened from his lapel. His eyes touched every face in the gallery, burned into every soul, making even the innocent squirm. When he was satisfied that conditions were right, he nodded at the court clerk, and the clerk intoned his call.

"Oyez, oyez, oyez. The Western District Circuit Court of the United States, Stone County, Missouri District, is now in session, the Honorable Judge Samuel Parkhurst Barnstall presiding."

The gallery was limited to fifty spectators, and tickets for attendance were as prized as tickets to a championship fight or a road show. Everyone knew that Judge Binder had run a crooked court. Now they were anxious to see what the new judge would do. There were some who expressed the belief that the only change would be new hands to take the bribe money. There were others, though, who had seen

Judge Barnstall up close, who had measured the set of his jaw, the glint of his eye. They insisted there was a new day coming and they wanted to be around to watch him handle his first case.

Judge Barnstall stepped through the same door Remington had come through. Though the judge wasn't as tall as Ned Remington, he was a robust man, with a square face and piercing blue eyes, so his presence was immediately felt. He moved quickly to the bench, then sat down.

"Be seated."

The gallery sat, then watched with interest as the prisoner was brought into the room for the trial.

The case for the prosecution was quick and simple. An Indian girl named Sister Blue Dress had been tending a store in Tahlequah. Two witnesses saw Amos Mordecai Cullimore come into the store and reach behind the counter for the moneybox. When Sister Blue Dress tried to pull the moneybox away from him, Cullimore shot her. She was killed with a .36-caliber bullet. Cullimore was carrying a .36-caliber Navy Colt when he was arrested.

Silas Lovelady, Cullimore's lawyer, called Lou Woods and Bill Sisley to testify for the defense. They both claimed that Cullimore had been with them on the day of the murder. Immediately after their testimony, Woods and Sisley were remanded into custody for murder charges not connected with the case at hand.

In his instructions to the jury Judge Barnstall said that Woods and Sisley were unreliable witnesses, whereas the two witnesses for the prosecution, a man and his daughter who had been in the store at the time, were known citizens of good character. The jury found Cullimore guilty.

After Cullimore's trial, Woods and Sisley were

tried and convicted in short order, despite the efforts of a court-appointed attorney named Gideon Ford. Cullimore's attorney, as amicus curiae, objected to the scheduling of the trial so quickly after Cullimore's, but Barnstall reminded him that "all prisoners are afforded a speedy trial."

Woods and Sisley were convicted by the same jury that had convicted Cullimore. Less than an hour after Judge Barnstall entered the courtroom, three men stood convicted for capital crimes. Reporters from Springfield, St. Joe, St. Louis, and Fort Smith were present in the courtroom and they sensed that something exceptional was about to happen. They had already commented on the swiftest justice they'd ever seen, and now they realized they might be writing history as a new era began.

"Bailiff, would you position the prisoners before the bench for sentencing, please?" Judge Barnstall said.

"Yes, Your Honor."

The three men were brought before the bench. Two of them stood with their heads bowed contritely. Cullimore stared defiantly at the judge while he passed sentence on Woods and Sisley, telling them both that they would die the next morning. Now it was Cullimore's time, and the judge turned toward him.

"Get it over with, Judge, I ain't got all day," Cullimore said. He giggled at his own joke.

"Amos Mordecai Cullimore," Judge Barnstall intoned, "in the morning, the sun will rise over these gentle Ozark hills and dispel the soft mist that has lain in these deep hollows all during the starry night. The air will become clean and fresh as the world awakens. The sun will turn the chill earth warm toward noon, but you won't be sitting down to lunch.

"The fish will jump in the ponds, race up the silver streams after nymphs, and frogs will croak on the banks. The dew will burn off the grasses and the morning glories will open their petals to the afternoon sun, but you won't be able to see any of this.

"The birds will sing from the treetops and the squirrels will scamper in the oaks and among the forest grasses. The honeybees will drink the sweet nectar of flowers and the hummingbirds sip the honeysuckle blossoms, but you will not be here to enjoy any of these things, Amos Mordecai Cullimore, because I hereby order the U.S. marshal to lead you to the gallows at ten of the clock tomorrow morning. There, the hangman will put a knotted noose around your neck and then pull the trapdoor lever, thereby dropping your filthy, raping, murdering, stealing carcass ten feet, where you will either break your neck or swing in the breeze. You will hang there as the townsfolk look at your miserable corpse, and then your worthless body will be cut down, placed in a crude pine box, and buried six feet underground in a potter's field where the worms and maggots can have free rein over what is left of your mortal body, you son of a bitch."

Chapter Two

The holding cell where the three condemned men were being detained was separated from the main jail. It was out in the side courtyard less than fifty feet from the gallows itself. No one was ever confined in the holding cells until the last few hours before execution. There, the condemned prisoners would be able to look through the barred windows and watch the crowd gather and the excitement grow as the time for their execution approached.

Lou Woods rolled his third quirly of the morning as Bill Sisley paced the eight feet of cell back and forth, dragging his irons, never looking at anything, just staring straight ahead as if the wall might melt away on his next turn and he could walk right through. Amos Cullimore lay on his back on the bunk, an arm thrown across his eyes. Outside, the sound of the pulley straining with the sandweight floated across the town square through the tiny barred window ten feet above where Woods squatted in the corner.

Sisley jumped and let out a little cry of alarm. Cullimore laughed, a dry, bitter laugh that could have come from hell.

"Don't you fret none, Bill, my boy! They're just greasin' the door to hell for you."

"Goddammit, Amos, you damned sure got us in a fix. I thought we killed that Injun boy what testified against us."

Sisley stopped pacing as if he had been jerked up short on the end of an invisible rope.

"Yeah," he growled, "we was supposed to be your alibi, not join you on the gallows."

Cullimore didn't move.

"You boys sit tight," he said. "You tell Nickerson to come like I said?"

"Yair, but we was goin' to help him after we done out witnessin'," said Lou.

"Tell him to bring horses, guns, and them two sourfaced cousins of his?"

"Yeah," drawled Sisley, "but they neither one got a brain between 'em. Logue Nickerson ain't much better."

Logan Nickerson was married to Cullimore's sister. His cousins, Elmo and Daryl Beale, were half-wits, but they did what Logue told them to do and they didn't care what it was. Lou Woods was a short, nervous man with shifty feral eyes, who, like Bill Sisley, did what Amos Cullimore told him to do. They were hollow men, left over after the war, who had fought on both sides, deserted both, and now roamed the lawless territories like scavengers, picking up what they could, taking what they wanted. To their surprise, they had been arrested when they entered Barnstall's courtroom, given a trial right along with Cullimore, and sentenced to hang this very morning.

"Logue knows what to do."

"Sounds like you didn't trust us much," said Sisley.

"Always good to have some insurance," Cullimore said. "Guess this here just proves my point."

"Shit," said Woods. "What's Logue going to do for me?"

"You wait," said Amos cryptically.

"Hell, I been waiting long enough," said Lou.

They all heard the trapdoor spring and the rope sing on the pulley before the sandbag hit the ground with a violent thud.

Lou threw his cigarette on the dirt floor of the cell and ground it to powder under his bootheel.

Ned Remington finished stalking the circumference of the town square and checked the deputies Sheriff Pat Cooper had placed in strategic places. Something was not quite right, but he couldn't put a finger to it. There were a lot of strange faces in town, some here on the square. The gallows stood in the center, its grisly shadow stretching under a rising sun. It was not quite nine o'clock, and yet the crowd was already thick, jostling for position. Barnstall had ordered the hanging to commence at ten sharp "so the people can get back to their business, talk about it over lunch. I'll recess at that time myself."

Remington carried the '73 Winchester, his pistol loose in its holster. Several hundred people were gathered around the gallows now. There were men in suits, shirt sleeves, and overalls, women in long dresses and bonnets, children threading in and out of the groups as they chased one another around the square. A few enterprising vendors passed through the crowd selling lemonade, beer, pretzels, popcorn, and sweet rolls. In one corner of the yard a black-frocked preacher stood on an overturned box, taking advantage of the situation to deliver a fiery sermon. The man was of average height and build, with a full head of thick black hair. Standing on the box, he jabbed his finger repeatedly toward the gallows as he harangued the crowd.

"In a few moments three creatures are going to be hurtled to eternity... sent to meet their Maker with blood on their hands and sin in their hearts."

He waggled his finger at the crowd. "And hear this now! Them three sinners is gonna be cast into hell, because not one of them, not a solitary one of them, has repented of their sins.

"It's too late for them, brothers 'n' sisters. They's all doomed to the fiery furnaces of hell, doomed to writhe in agony forever!"

Some of those who were close enough to hear the preacher shivered involuntarily at his powerful imagery and looked toward the gallows. One or two of them touched their necks fearfully, and a few souls, perhaps weak on willpower, sneaked a drink from a bottle.

"It's too late for them, but it's not too late for you! Repent! Repent now, I say, for the wages of sin is death and eternal damnation!"

The preacher's voice carried well and was certainly heard by the three men in the holding cell. At the window of the cell a face would sometimes appear, look nervously though the bars at the crowd, then withdraw to the gloomy shadows within. A couple of young boys approached the cell and tried to peer in through the window, but a woman called out to them and they returned to the crowd.

On the second floor of the courtroom, Judge Barnstall stood at the window of his chambers and looked down on the proceedings. He beckoned for the marshal to come up, and Ned touched a finger to the flat brim of his hat.

Logan Nickerson watched the tall marshal cross the square and enter the court building. He looked at the Beale brothers, who had the Springfield wagon backed up to the dry-goods store, around the corner. Under the cloth that was spread over the bed, there were five rifles, three scatterguns, and six pistols, all loaded. They wore no arms in sight. The dark-haired man looked like just another farmer in coveralls, a peaked hat on his head, a piece of straw between his teeth. His face was pockmarked, pinched around a pair of small, deep-sunk eyes. He had tagged every deputy's position, had it all planned out. In the alley behind the store, six horses stood hipshot in the shade, saddled and ready to ride.

Remington knocked on the door of Barnstall's office. A voice told him to come in.

"Anything unusual?" the judge asked as Remington stepped inside.

"No, should there be?"

"Cullimore doesn't want to hang, I think he's got help. He did this once before. He wasn't sentenced to hang, but he promised to give himself up to a sheriff over in Monett. Came in unarmed, as agreed.

Sheriff had two deputies with him. One of them got away alive."

"What happened?"

"Cullimore had some friends who waited for them in town, shot the sheriff down, brought Cullimore a horse. No one tried to stop them."

"Know who they were? His friends?"

Barnstall shook his head.

"So what now, Sam? Cooper's got deputies all over. We've got Dan Norling, the Swede, up on the courthouse roof, and Kurt Hammer is standing in the shade of the gallows."

"Good, but I've got an idea. Bring them into the jail. I think they're about the right size."

"What?"

Barnstall arose from behind his cherrywood desk.

"I'll meet you at the jail, tell you the rest of it there."

At the jail, Sisley and Woods were called out, told to strip down to their underwear. Hammer and Norling dressed in their clothes. Cullimore was kept in the dark. At nine forty-five, the men started the walk to the gallows, with Cullimore following behind the two disguised deputies. Remington was in the lead. Norling and Hammer kept their leads low, and the flanking deputies pretty much concealed them from Cullimore's scrutiny.

Just as they reached the scaffold, Nickerson and the Beale brothers made their move. They took shotguns from the wagon and shot down the sheriff's deputies. People screamed and ran for cover. There was a lot of smoke and confusion. After the scatter guns were empty, the three men turned their rifles onto the crowd and began firing.

Remington shoved Cullimore under the scaffold. Norling and Hammer broke away, enclosing the Nickerson bunch in a pincer movement. As the three men ran toward the gallows, the two marshals cut them down. Cullimore struggled to break free, but Remington rammed his .44 New Model Army pistol barrel halfway down his throat, cocking the hammer. He didn't need to say a word.

Five minutes later, with Woods and Sisley rejoining Cullimore, the three men were led to the gallows. Their legs were no longer hobbled, but their hands were handcuffed behind their backs. Lou Woods, who had been smoking, spit out his quirly just as they reached the foot of the stairs with its thirteen steps.

Bill Sisley was leading the group, and he hesitated at the first step.

"Lou?" he said in a small, frightened voice.

"Go on up there," Lou replied. "You done your killin' like a man—take your punishment like one."

"It just don't seem right. We was supposed to help Cullimore, not get hung with him."

The three men stepped onto the scaffold; then the hangman positioned them under the nooses that dangled from the crossbeam. From there the condemned prisoners had a good view of the crowd.

Bill couldn't look into the faces of the spectators, and he closed his eyes. He trembled as he stood there. Lou and Cullimore stared ahead blankly, as if looking at something far beyond the crowd.

The preacher came up the steps then and approached each man.

"Do you want to repent?" he asked each in turn.

Lou and Cullimore made no answer at all. Bill tried to speak, but no words would come. Finally he nodded, and the preacher put his hand on Bill's shoulder and said a few quiet words that only he could hear. Finally the preacher stopped praying and stepped to one side.

"Any last words, gentlemen?" the hangman asked.

Cullimore was the only one of the three to speak.

"You ladies out there," he said, "I hope you enjoy this. I've always been one that tried to give the ladies their pleasure."

There was a gasp of indignation from the crowd, and the hangman stepped up quickly.

"All right, you've had your say. It's time." He put a black hood over Cullimore's head, then fit his noose. The hangman placed the hood and noose on each of the others in turn.

Bill was shaking visibly.

"When the trap opens, don't hunch up your shoulders," the hangman said. "Just relax and you'll die quick. It's better that way."

"I'll . . . I'll try," Bill mumbled through the hood.

"Get on with it," Cullimore rasped through his hood. "Tell Barnstall I'll be waitin' in hell for him."

When the hangman had them all ready, he stepped over to the handle that would open the trapdoor. He glanced up toward the window where Judge Barnstall stood looking down. Barnstall nodded his head, and the hangman pulled the handle.

The long trapdoor swung down on its hinges and the three bodies dropped about ten feet. There was a gasp from the crowd as the bodies fell.

Lou and Bill died instantly. They hit the end of their drop, then just swung and twirled. But Cullimore was still alive, and for almost four minutes he kept drawing his body up as if in that way he could relieve the weight on his neck. His stomach heaved, and those nearest the scaffold could hear rasping sounds from his throat. Finally his body, like the others, was still.

Chapter Three

In the stores and around the supper tables of Galena that night, people spoke of the swift justice that had been dispensed by Judge Barnstall's court. The saloon crawlers who moved from the bright lights of one saloon through the shadows of the dark streets and into the bright lights of another saloon took the stories and the gossip with them, so that the entire main street became a buzz of excitement. The town loafers, sitting on benches in front of the hotel or on the edges of the boardwalks near the corner lamps, whittled and speculated about the changes the new judge had already brought about. Everyone agreed that the triple hanging they had witnessed that day was more excitement than Galena had ever known.

Ned Remington moved along the board sidewalk, heading for Judge Barnstall's office. Though he was a big man, he was light on his feet and the boards made little noise as he passed along the street, now illuminated by a golden spill of light from a window or door, now practically invisible in the shadows of darkness. A cacophony of sound washed through the night: half a dozen pianos and as many different songs, a man's loud voice, a woman's shrill laughter, the hollow clop of horses' hooves on the dirt street, the happy shout of kids playing kick the can. It was a town vital and alive ... and, for the most part, law-abiding.

Ned passed the gallows, standing dark and silent now that it had done its gruesome duty. When he reached the courthouse he climbed the steps to Judge Barnstall's second-floor office, then knocked on the door.

"Come on in, Ned," Barnstall called.

Ned pushed the door open and stepped inside. There were several papers spread out on Barnstall's desk, three open books, and a full inkwell. Barnstall put down his pen and pointed to the liquor cabinet, on which stood two glasses and a bottle. Ned pulled the cork and poured a drink for each of them.

"Working late," he said.

"It's the way of things," Barnstall replied. "We'll be working six days a week—Sundays off if the outlaws let us take off—from nine in the morning until whenever I bang my gavel at the end of the day."

Ned looked around the judge's office. It was small, neat, lined with bookshelves chock-full of lawbooks. On one wall was a map of the western United States, and another, on parchment, of the Indian Nations. There was a framed law degree from Harvard, a globe on a walnut stand, leather chairs, the mahogany liquor cabinet, with, in addition to the bottle of bourbon Ned had poured the drink from, a brandy decanter and a set of snifters. On the desk where the judge had been working, there was a stack of foolscap next to the wooden pen he had been using. The judge's name was etched on a wooden plaque, and on another the legend *Ignorantia legis neminem excusat.*

Judge Barnstall held his glass toward Ned, not in a toast as such, but rather as a quiet salute. He tossed the drink down, then picked up the bottle Ned had put on the desk and poured himself another one.

"We got us a problem here, Ned," he said. He tossed a sheaf of warrants in the marshal's lap. "Four men waylaid a farmer and his family south of here, raped and killed the women, slit the farmer's throat. Only a boy got away, and he positively identified the assailants, who will hereafter be referred to as scum."

Ned looked over the warrants.

"I don't see any problem here. These men all live in Kirbyville or Hollister. They took a fair amount of cash as well as some goods. Looks like the local sheriff could handle it."

"They killed the Hollister constable when he tried to serve a local warrant." He paused as Ned flipped papers. "Next page, paragraph six, in the addenda."

"How did this land in your court's jurisdiction?"

"The farmer was from Reeds Spring. He sold his stock at the auction in Springfield, was moving down to the White River valley when they jumped him. Look at the victims' names again."

"Jefferson Parkhurst, deceased; Marilyn Louise Parkhurst, deceased, wife of Jefferson; and Cathryn Parkhurst, daughter of..." Ned stopped reading and sucked in a breath. He looked at the judge with stone-gray eyes. "Why, isn't this...?"

"My dear departed uncle, Ned. Jeff Parkhurst was

my mother's brother, dearly beloved of her, and I want those scum up here before my bench so I can make the sweat stream off their balls before I sentence them to the gallows."

"You pushed a lot for this one, Judge. I don't see any federal laws—"

"There's plenty of law here to back this up, dammit. Kidnapping, child molesting, crossing state lines in the commission of a crime. Let me worry about the law."

"Says here they were killed south of Kirbyville at a place called Murderer's Rocks. That's in Missouri."

"Just barely. Another five or six miles and they'd have been in Arkansas. Maybe they took my cousin Cathryn down there to..." The judge's jaw clenched and his eyes sparked blue fire as he curled a fist around the shot glass in his hand.

"The boy a good witness?"

"Jedediah is at my home."

"Christ, Sam, you're really stretching things here."

"Ned, just bring those bat-toothed, bowlegged, gaul-fisted, suck-egg sons of bitches in to my court."

Ned downed his drink, then stood up, his fingers working the brim of his hat.

"No problem, Sam."

"Yes, Ned, there is a problem. These scum, Jacob Newsome, Ephraim Flatt, Thomas Gerner, and William Kimmons, are all ex–border guerrillas. They fought with Quantrill and Bloody Bill Anderson, rode with Alf Bolin and some others. They know the country. They're crack shots, and each one of 'em's meaner than a snake-bit mule."

"I'll take care of it personally, then."

"Don't try and do it by yourself. Take some of your deputies with you."

"I will," Ned said.

"How soon do you plan to get started?"

"I'll get started first thing tomorrow. I, uh, may send Jim Early to round up a couple of the deputies for me. I want to pay a little visit to someone first."

Barnstall looked at his marshal for a moment, then stroked his chin. "Yes," he said, "I guess this does sort of remind you of your own case, doesn't it? You understand, then, why I want these men?"

"Yeah," Ned said quietly. "I understand."

Later that same night, Jim Early, a small, wiry man who was leather-tough and whipcord fast, rode into a clearing in the Ozark woods. Jim was Ned's most reliable deputy, and when Ned asked him to round up a couple of the men Jim didn't even ask who he was to get. He knew that Ned had full trust and confidence in him to take care of the situation. He didn't ask Ned where he would be, either. He knew the answer to that question too.

Jim stopped his horse just inside the clearing and patted the animal's neck. He called out to the log cabin set back a ways in the clearing. A man appeared out of the shadows and told Jim to light down from his horse. From the man's sudden appearance Jim knew that his approach hadn't been a secret, though he had ridden as quietly as he could.

"Been a time," Tom Beck said.

"Can we go inside?"

"Afraid of wolves, Jim?"

"Got something for you to read."

The short, harsh laugh was not lost on Early.

Inside the tiny cabin, by the light of a dingy oil

lamp, Beck looked at the papers. He could read, but just barely. It took him a long time to sort it out. Early said nothing. It was just too painful to watch the ex-muleskinner, trapper, buffalo-skinner, ex-hardcase, go over the official papers. Beck had steely blue eyes, hair straight as straw with a tinge of red, a sharp, hooked nose. There wasn't an ounce of fat on his lean, spare frame. He was short, but he took advantage of that in a fight, and many a big man had gone down under his flailing fists or boots. He didn't know what wasn't fair in a fight, but he had a solid rule: Hit first, hit hard, and keep hitting until the opponent gave up or his lamp went out. Remington had found him in Taos, working as a deputy sheriff, learned he had done the same at Tombstone, Dodge, Ellsworth. The man was a tracker and he didn't give up. He had endeared himself to sheriffs because he didn't back down and he didn't mind going on long hard trails by himself.

"I knowed one of these Arkies," Beck said finally. "Bill Kimmons. And I seen Jake Newsome in a knife fight down to Fort Smith oncet. He come out on top. What'd they do?"

Early told him.

"You goin'?"

"No. Ned's takin' this one himself. I won't be goin' along."

"Where's Ned at now?"

"He had a call to make," Early said without elaboration. "I want you to get McKirk in on this."

"Reckon that Scottie will ride with us?"

"You tell him Ned wants him."

"Yeah," Beck said. "Reckon just about any of us would go if Ned said he wanted us. How come you ain't goin'?"

"Ned wants me to stay aroun' 'case Barnstall needs anything."

"That who I'm workin' for?"

"Ned works for him. You and me, we're workin' for Ned. Stand up, Tom."

"What for?"

"I'm going to deputize you."

"Well, I'll be damned. A U.S. marshal."

"Yeah, maybe," Jim said wryly as he began to swear in Tom Beck. "If this ain't quite official, I guess Ned can make it so when you start out." Jim started for the door. "You get the Scot... I'll go back and tell Ned his deputies will be ready by tomorrow."

"I'll get him come sunup," Tom said. "I don't cotton to goin' up to his place in the middle of the night."

Jim smiled. "Can't say as I blame you any," he agreed.

John Angus McKirk worked as a shotgun for the local freight outfits that drove from Springfield to Harrison, Arkansas. When he felt like it. The rest of the time he fished and hunted in the Ozark woods. He played the bagpipes when he was going through one of his periodic episodes of melancholy, but few knew that. He lived alone, in the backwoods near the White River as it wandered along the border, and few had been there. He had worked as a U.S. marshal before, but had resigned after one of his partners committed suicide when they were pinned down by Comanches. It had left him badly rattled, but he had managed to shoot his way out. Few would work with him after that. He was taciturn as stone, cold as cave ice, mean as a timber rattler shedding its skin. He was sensitive about his broad burr and hid a lot of his feelings behind a reddish beard that gave him the look of an enraged Moses when his cobalt-blue eyes flashed in anger.

He was tall, thin, angular, fond of wearing a dark waistcoat and knee-high black boots. He wore a double-rig six-gun harness and was plumb-center good with either hand. Some said he kept a girl at his place to cook his meals for him, but no one ever saw her. If he had one, she was as shy as a whippoorwill.

Tom Beck called from the crest of the wagon road about a quarter mile from the cabin.

"Ho, John Angus, it's Tom Beck."

Tom sat his Indian pony and waited. He peered hard at the cabin below, hoping to catch a glimpse of the girl he'd heard tell about. He'd been here a half-dozen times and never seen her, but he still looked. The cabin was shut up tight as a widow's purse, and there was no smoke from its chimney. A pair of kid goats chewed at an old horsehair rope, and he heard the squawk of a chicken from the henhouse. It sounded like someone drawing a knife blade over slate. A small creek meandered back of the cabin, and there was a line of clothes, all male duds, fluttering between two willow trees.

Ten minutes later, the cabin door opened a crack and McKirk stepped out, shading his eyes from the sun, which was just above the eastern horizon, behind Beck's back. He wore the dark waistcoat, was hatless. Although he couldn't have been much more than thirty or so, his pate was bald except for the flanking rust hair that was curly as a wolf's mane. He wore a bright red flannel shirt under the dark coat, and Tom saw the twin butts of his ugly Colt's hoglegs flaring against the lining.

"Wha' in the name of the eternal Christ do ye want wi' a mon at thus vurry earrly hour, Tom Beck?"

"U.S. business, John Angus. Ned Remington sent me, said for you to come. You can read these papers whilst you go for your horse. Bring some grub. We may be a while."

John Angus fixed Beck with a fierce scowling look as he stepped close and snatched the papers out of his hand. He nodded toward the cabin, and the other man understood. McKirk wasn't going to walk back down there with his back to the man, no matter what. Beck knew McKirk, didn't like to be around him. He made a man spooky. Too moody, Tom said when others asked him, but that wasn't it. McKirk seldom said what was on his mind, and when he did it never was what anyone expected. He kept his thoughts to himself, and it was sometimes nerve-racking.

"Set on that kindling stump. Be wi' ye by and by."

When the Scotsman joined Beck, mounted on a rangy Tennessee roan, a brace of extra pistols dangling from his saddle horn, Tom tossed him a shiny object.

"Wha' ye..."

"I'll swear you in as we ride, John Angus. Tell you like Jim Early told me. If this ain't official, I reckon Ned can make it right."

John Angus regarded the badge with a baleful eye, pinned it on his coat reluctantly.

As the two men topped the rise Beck looked back at the clothes still hanging on the line.

"Forgot to ask if you wanted to take your clothes down before we left, John Angus. Might not be there when you get back."

"Aye, dinna fret yoursel' aboot thut, Tom. If the goats don't eat them, they'll be taken keer of, laddie."

Beck suppressed a smile as the two of them rode over the hill, three days' rations in their saddlebags, bedrolls tied behind their cantles, and guns loaded, spare ammunition in their pockets.

Chapter Four

Jim Early dismounted outside the walls of the convent, tied his horse at the hitching rail, then pulled on the rope that hung alongside the gate. He heard the bell ring, and a few moments later the gate was opened by a young nun. She smiled when she recognized Jim.

"Deputy Early," she said. "How nice to see you."

"Hello, Sister Angela," Jim said. "How is your Mother Superior?"

"She is well, thank you."

"I wonder if I could speak with her."

"Of course. She will be very pleased to see you," Sister Angela said. "Won't you come this way?"

Jim followed the nun through the garden of the convent. It was well shaded and alive with flowering plants of all descriptions. A fountain bubbled in the middle of the garden pool, and birds, instinctively knowing this was a sanctuary, flitted from branch to statue to birdbath. A well-worn path of stone led from the garden to Mother Superior's office.

Mother Superior was a robust and healthy-looking seventy-year-old. She got up from her desk and shuffled around quickly to greet Jim. A broad smile spread across her face.

"James!" she said. "It is so good to see you."

Jim stuck his hand in his inside jacket pocket and pulled out a small package.

"I brought something for you."

"Licorice! How nice!"

"How do you know it's licorice?"

Mother Superior smiled. "Because you know I have a taste for the confection," she said. "And you've not yet learned that you don't have to come bearing gifts. You are welcome here anytime, James."

"I know I don't have to come bearing gifts, Mother Superior," Jim said. "But when Ned Remington brought me here, shot to pieces... nearly dead, you took me in and treated me as if I were one of you."

"You *are* one of us, James. We're all God's children," Mother Superior said.

"I'll never forget you for your kindness to me... or to Ned's Katy."

A shadow passed across Mother Superior's eyes.

"Ah, the poor girl," she said. "I'm afraid she has wounds that all the medicinal skills of the world can't heal. Even a father's love can't make her well again."

"Has there been no change at all?"

"I'm afraid not," Mother Superior said. "Bless her heart, she just sits there in that shell of hers, staring out at the world through those terrible, tortured eyes.

She speaks to no one, not even her father. I don't think she knows who he is. Sometimes I think the poor girl doesn't even know who *she* is."

"I don't know where Ned would be without you and the sisters to look out for her," Jim said.

"We do what we can, but it's too little, I'm afraid. My only hope now is that we don't lose Marshal Remington as well."

"What do you mean?"

"Sometimes when he is here visiting his daughter, I look in the room and see the two of them there. They each seem to be lost in their own world. The poor girl, bless her, has eyes which are tortured. But the eyes of the father... they are cold and dangerous, James. Oh, I don't mean to me or to any of the sisters. There's never been a man who could be more gentle than Ned Remington, to his daughter or to us, you know that. Why, you remember that after he brought you here, Marshal Remington came every day until you were out of danger."

"Yeah," Jim said. "I know." He recalled those times when he would surface from his wound-induced deep sleep to see Ned standing over his bed. He couldn't hold on to consciousness for any period of time, and for a while he didn't know if Ned was really there or if he was merely a hallucination.

"Those same eyes which fill me with such foreboding on some occasions are full of love and compassion when he's looking at his daughter, or some other poor soul in need of comfort. But"—Mother Superior shivered involuntarily—"though he doesn't speak of it, I know that his heart is consumed by a terrible passion to kill other fellow human beings ... the man, or men, who did that awful thing to Katy and his wife."

"Can you blame him, Mother Superior? Someone raped and killed Ned's wife, then raped Katy and left her for dead. He left her worse than dead, for Katy is now a living dead. She doesn't speak, laugh, cry... she doesn't even recognize Ned. When Ned came back and found what had happened to his wife... his daughter, it nearly killed him."

"I agree," Mother Superior said. "It is an awful thing for a man to live with. I sometimes don't know what has kept him going."

"I'll tell you what's kept him going," Jim said. "It's the thought of finding out who it was and bringing him to justice."

"But he mustn't dwell on that," Mother Superior said. "That lust for revenge is contrary to God's law. 'Vengeance is mine,' said the Lord," Mother Superior said.

"Not vengeance, Mother Superior... justice. There is a difference. And in the Stone County Federal District, we have another law. 'Justice is mine,' saith Judge Samuel Parkhurst Barnstall," Jim replied.

"Do you really thing there is a difference between justice and vengeance?" Mother Superior asked.

"There is a difference," Jim said. "But sometimes vengeance can be served by justice."

"I have heard that Judge Barnstall is a very hard man. Is it true that he sent three men to the gallows yesterday?"

"Yes, Mother Superior. But never have three men deserved such a fate more than they."

"I pray for the day when justice can be administered with a more gentle hand," Mother Superior said. "But I do understand that there is a proper place and time for the sword of Gideon."

"This is such a time, Mother Superior. Four men killed and raped a farmer's family."

Mother Superior looked up. "James, are they the same ones?"

"I don't know. But the man who was murdered was Judge Barnstall's uncle. It may not be the same people who murdered Ned's wife, but Ned understands the pain Judge Barnstall feels. And when he brings these men in, vengeance will be served by justice."

"Yes, I can see why Ned might want to go after these men. Do you know where they went?" Mother Superior asked.

"We don't know, but they have to be somewhere close. They haven't had time to get too far away."

"I just pray that Mr. Remington's judgment is not impaired by thinking of his own sorrow," Mother Superior said.

"Have no fear about Ned's judgment, or his skills," Jim said. "He is the perfect man for this job."

"I suppose so. Still, when I look into Katy's room and see him sitting there, so gentle, so loving with his daughter, it is hard to imagine him as a man who could deal with the violence of such men as you have described. I suppose you have come for him?"

"Yes."

"He's in his daughter's room. He's been with her since early this morning. Would you like one of the sisters to show you the way?"

"No," Jim said. "I can find it."

As Jim started to leave he saw Mother Superior looking at the package of licorice he had brought her. He smiled. "Go ahead, have a piece now," he said, smiling.

REMINGTON 41

Mother Superior put it on her desk.

"No," she said. "Not until after vespers. If I'm to give in to a vice, I shall at least keep it under control."

Jim chuckled. "Whatever you say."

He walked down a long corridor to the last door on the right. He saw that the door was ajar, so he pushed it open quietly and looked inside.

The room was dark. Katy sat in a rocking chair on one side of the room, rocking slowly, staring blankly off into space with those terrible frightened eyes Mother Superior had spoken of. She was humming a tuneless little song.

On the opposite side of the room, standing there and looking out the window, Jim saw his boss, U.S. Marshal Ned Remington. From this angle a beam of light splashed through the window, and Jim could see that the cold, steely eyes that had been the last thing on earth more than one gunfighter had seen were now covered with a light sheen of moisture.

Tears?

It was not something any sane man would ever want to point out to Ned Remington.

Jim cleared his throat.

"Yeah, Jim," Ned called. He looked toward his deputy. "Did you take care of things?"

"Tom Beck and John Angus McKirk," Jim said. "They'll be in town today, ready to go."

Ned walked over to the bed and picked up his hat. "Good. I promised Judge Barnstall I'd have his prisoners back within a week."

"How is she?" Jim asked, nodding toward the young girl in the rocking chair. He knew how she was, hated himself for asking, but he felt that some recognition of her was required.

Ned looked across the room at his daughter. He was silent for a long moment before he spoke.

"Katy," he said. "How old would you say she is?"

"I . . . I wouldn't say," Jim replied.

"She's twenty-one," Ned said. "Twenty-one and beautiful. By rights she should be married by now and I should be a grandpa. But look at her, Jim. She's a child. My beautiful, smart, wonderful daughter is twenty-one and a child. No, not even a child, because when she was a child she could at least talk to me. When she was a baby her face would light up with a smile every time she saw me, or her . . . her mother," Ned added painfully. He sighed. "She can't even do that now. She can't even smile."

Jim stood holding his hat in his hand, turning it slowly.

"I'm sorry," he said awkwardly.

"No," Ned said. "No, *I'm* sorry. I had no right to burden you with this. It isn't your problem, it's mine." He stood up and walked over to Katy, kissed her lightly on the cheek, then smiled at Jim. "I know the men I'm going after are probably not the ones who did this to Mary and Katy. But I've no doubt that they would have done it if they had the opportunity. So you can understand when I say I'm going to take particular pleasure in bringing these bastards in."

Chapter Five

The town of Hollister had 104 inhabitants and two principal streets which formed a V where Turkey Creek began its final run before flowing into the White River. The town was made up of the usual collection of private residences and business establishments. Some of the buildings, by their substantial construction, showed a faith in the future of the town. Others, thrown together from wood scraps and canvas, indicated that the owners were less sure and were ready to move on at a moment's notice.

The Bank at Hollister, built of brick, occupied a position right at the intersection of the two streets. Right across from it was a hotel, made of wood, two stories high, with a second-story balcony that ran all the way around the building. Below the balcony, at street level, was a fine wooden porch with a dozen rocking chairs, half of which were occupied when Remington, Beck, and McKirk rode into town.

A large painted sign hung over the porch, advertising the hotel rooms as the "most luxurious in the county." The sign swung gently in the late-afternoon breeze and its squeaking could be heard all up and down the street. Just down the street from the hotel was Ma Morgan's Restaurant, and next door to that, the Red Lion Tavern.

"Let's ask a few questions," Ned said, and the three men dismounted in front of the hotel. Ned handed Beck the reins to his horse while he stepped up onto the porch. The man nearest him spit a quid into a spittoon that sat on the porch, then wiped his mouth with the back of his hand. He was a man in his sixties with a long gray beard and a stained hat, pulled low over dark eyes. He looked up at Ned.

"I'm Marshal Ned Remington, riding for Judge Barnstall's court out of Galena."

"Marshal," the man said.

"I'm looking for four men. Could be that they're right here in Hollister."

"I wouldn't know."

"Their names are—" Ned started, but one of the others interrupted him.

"Marshal, it won't do no good to give us names. Don't none of us know a soul what ain't from right here in town."

"What if these men are from Hollister?" Ned asked.

"Then we wouldn't be likely to help you bring in one of our own, would we?"

"You'd be doing the law a favor."

"Don't owe the law no favors," one of the men said.

Ned looked around at Beck and McKirk, standing on the porch just behind him. He could get angry, threaten these loafers, but if he got information that way, how reliable would it be? He sighed and turned away from them.

"What'd they do?" the first man asked.

"Does it matter?"

"It might. Iffen they took railroad money, or money from a Yankee bank, then I say more power to 'em."

"They murdered a farmer's family," Ned said. "But not until after they let him watch them rape his wife and daughter."

One of the other men squirted out a stream of tobacco and then leaned back in his chair to cut a new plug. "Why'n't you say that in the first place?" he asked.

"Didn't figure it made any difference."

"It does. Son of a bitches like that needs to be caught, no matter who they be."

"Yeah," one of the others said. "Iffen you catch up with the bastards I hope you're aimin' to shoot 'em."

"I'm going to take them back to Judge Barnstall's court and let him hang them," Ned said.

"Hangin's too good for 'em. You ought to shoot 'em down like dogs."

"No, I agree with the marshal," the first man said. "A bullet's too quick. You ever see a man hang? See the veins pop out on his neck and in his arms? See him kick and squirm at the end of a rope? Hangin's just what these fellas need."

"What were them names again?"

"William Kimmons, Thomas Gerner, Jacob Newsome, and Ephraim Flatt," Ned said. "The names mean anything to you?"

The six men went into a conference, talking

quietly among themselves for a moment; then the first one cleared his throat.

"Ain't them the same ones shot down Constable Miller last week?"

"Yes," Ned said.

"I thought as much."

"Do you know where they might be now?"

"Old man Newsome owns a farm beyond Kirbyville, near Blackwell's Ferry Road. He's got a boy named Jake. Reckon that's one of your men."

"You know this fella Jake?" Ned asked.

The old man squirted out another stream of tobacco juice. "Yeah, I know him."

"Have you seen him around? Do you know if he's here?"

"I ain't seen him, but that don't mean nothin'. Jake never was the sociable type. Truth is, he could be right out there at his pa's house and most folks in town would never know it."

"I see. Thanks," Ned said. "Thanks for your help."

Ned and the others remounted, rode fifty yards down the street until they came to the Red Lion Tavern. They tied their horses to the hitchrail, then, with three pair of boots clomping across the wooden sidewalk, shoved past the batwing doors and stepped inside. The saloon walls, the floor, the stairs leading up to the second floor, and the bar were constructed of raw unfinished wood. Behind the bar there was a long mirror, and above the mirror a painting of a reclining, fleshy girl in harem pajamas.

An out-of-tune piano was grinding away at the back of the tavern. There were men at the bar and more at the half-dozen tables. Card games were going on at two of the tables, but the stakes were low and the laughter and banter that came from the players indicated that no one was taking the game very seriously. A girl was standing by the piano, leaning against the wall, looking out over the floor. She smiled when the three men first came in, started toward them, noticed the badges, then stopped and retreated to the piano.

Ned and the others stepped up to the bar.

"What'll it be, gents?" the barkeep asked, running a damp cloth over the bar in front of them.

Ned and Beck ordered beer, McKirk a scotch.

"Would you know if Jake Newsome is around?" Ned asked conversationally.

"You a friend of his?"

"No."

"Then why are you looking for him?"

"We want to ask him a few questions," Ned said. It wasn't until that moment that the bartender noticed the badges.

"Oh," he said. "Well, he ain't no friend of mine, that's for sure."

"Then you don't mind telling us where we can find him."

"He might be out to his ol' man's place," the bartender said. "Charlie would know more about that than me."

"Charlie? Who's Charlie?"

"Charlie Bell," the bartender said. He pointed to a man standing at the far end of the bar. The man was of medium height, in his fifties, bald-headed. He was nursing a drink, taking very small sips to make it last a long time. "Charlie works for ol' man Newsome sometimes."

"Give him another of whatever he's drinking," Ned said as he moved down the bar toward Charlie.

"Howdy, Marshal," Charlie said before Ned opened his mouth. "Figured you fellas would be comin' after Jake sooner or later."

"Why?"

"The old man said his boy and that bunch he runs with, Flatt, Gerner, and Kimmons, got into a little mischief last week."

"If you call killing a constable mischief," Ned said.

"They're sayin' that was self-defense. They've even got a few witnesses who'll stand up for 'em."

"It doesn't matter," Ned said. "That's not why I'm after them. Are they out at Newsome's house?" The new drink was put before Charlie, and he picked it up.

"You didn't have to buy me this, you know. I was gonna tell you ever'thin' I know anyway. Jake ain't no account, never has been, never will be. I can't stay out there and work while he's aroun'. I'd just as soon he be gone to jail somewhere. Be better for the old man, too, but you can't get him to see that. He's blind as a bat when it comes to gettin' him to understand what a rotten lout his boy is."

"I guess some folks just got a blind spot that way," Beck suggested.

"How about it, mon?" McKirk asked, his frustration making the brogue more pronounced. "Would you answer the marshal's question?"

"You're Scotch, ain't you? Fought in the war with a Scotchman. Good man he was, too." Charlie tossed the new drink down, not bothering to nurse this one as he had the other. "Jake's out there," he said. "He's there, but the other three have gone back down to Arkansas. Fact is, Jake normally lives down there with them. He's just up visitin' his pa."

"If we get him, we'll find out where the others are," Beck said.

"It ain't gonna be that easy to get any of them," Charlie said. "They're always armed. Hell, Jake don't go to the outhouse without he's got a gun with him. He's a good shot and as mean as they come. He could gut a man as easy as another man might gut a fish."

"It doesn't matter," Ned said. "We're going after him."

Chapter Six

Had the three men been making the ride for any other purpose, they might have taken the time to enjoy the beauty of the gentle Ozark hills. The road itself began alongside a wild and rushing stream whose surface was frothed white when tumbling over the rocks, clear and silver when running free. A short distance from town, the road began to climb, and they crossed another creek, which the locals named Coon, and mounted a wide, flat ridge. Cardinals and bluebirds flitted among the dogwood trees while monarch butterflies floated just above a field of daisies. The hills were dappled green and brown in close, blue and purple as they marched off into the distance. Here and there a large jut of rock would lift itself from the verdant growth around it, showing the remains of the cataclysmic fault that had created the Ozark Mountains at the dawn of the ages.

They smelled the wood smoke before they saw it,

spread out in a haze over a small meadow. Beneath the cloud of smoke was a house, one that had obviously been expanded in size over the years. The center part of the house was the oldest; then, protruding from both ends, there were added rooms. Because of the difference in the weathering of the wood it was easy to see where one construction left off and another began.

Ned signaled a stop and the three riders sat astride their horses for a moment, looking down on the pastoral scene. The smell of cooking meat mingled with the smell of wood smoke, and they heard someone's loud laugh.

"'Pears like they're about to sit to supper," Beck observed.

"Aye, and better than the fare we had a bit ago, I'm thinkin'," McKirk put in.

The back door to the house opened and a woman stepped onto the porch, threw out a pan of water, then went back inside.

"Damn," Ned swore. "There's a woman in that house ... maybe kids."

"What are we gonna do, Ned?"

Ned rubbed his chin for a moment, then pointed to the tree line around the clearing.

"You two move on up as close as you can get without being seen. I'll ride on down in the open, call him out. Maybe if he thinks I'm the only one here he'll come out."

Beck and McKirk nodded; then, with Beck leading the way, the two deputies moved down to get into position. With his knees, Ned urged his horse down toward the cabin.

Maybe this wasn't the right person, he thought. This was obviously a family gathering, kinfolk sitting down to supper together. It seemed unlikely that a man who was close to his kin could brutally murder an entire family the way Jake Newsome was supposed to have done. Those kinds of men tended to be loners... people who didn't fit in society. How could such a person be here in this house?

The front door opened and a man came outside when Ned was no closer than sixty feet. The man was tall and thin, with a long, narrow gray beard and long, stringy hair. He was holding a shotgun loosely by his side, and he spit out a stream of tobacco juice as Ned approached.

"That's close enough, mister," the man said.

"Would you be Mr. Newsome?"

"I would be. And this here is my land. What are you doing on it?"

"Mr. Newsome, my name is Ned Remington. I'm a U.S. marshal. I've come to see your son, Jake."

"Jake don't live here no more," Newsome said. "He lives across the border, down in Arkansas."

Ned saw a curtain in the window move, caught sight of a gun barrel just on the ledge.

"Would you have any idea where in Arkansas I might find him?"

"Naw. He don't live in no one place. He sort of wanders around a mite," Newsome said.

"I see," Ned said. He touched the brim of his hat. "I thank you for your time, Mr. Newsome."

Ned turned to ride away. If he hadn't been sure before that Jake was in the house, seeing the gun at the window convinced him. There was nothing to do now but spread the three of them around the house and keep an eye open. Jake couldn't stay in there forever. When he tried to leave, they'd get him.

Suddenly Ned heard the crashing of glass. He

didn't have to think twice about what it was. He felt the hackles rise on the back of his neck. With a shout to his horse he bent low over the neck and slapped his legs hard against the animal's side. The horse bolted forward just as the sound of the gunshot reached him. A bullet whistled inches over his head. Had he not been bending over at just that moment, the bullet would have hit Ned in the back of the head.

"You ignernt fool! What the hell are you shootin' at him for?" Newsome shouted to the ambusher. "There'll be hell to pay now, and there's women and kids in this house!"

Newsome's admonition to the gunman bought Ned just enough time to gain the tree line. Barely. From the moment he dismounted there was more shooting from the house, and Ned heard the bullets snap and pop as the missiles flew through the limbs and leaves of the trees.

"You all right, laddie?" McKirk called.

"Yes," Ned shouted back. "Tom...John Angus ...spread out," he called. "Don't let him sneak out of there."

Someone in the house opened up with a shotgun. The gun roared and smoke billowed, but the charge of shot was spent by the time it reached the woodline, and Ned could hear the pellets falling, rattling like sleet on dry leaves.

"Ned...should we shoot back?" Beck called.

"We can't! There are women and kids inside," Ned answered.

No sooner had Ned spoken than he heard McKirk's rifle bark. At first Ned started to yell at him; then he saw what McKirk was doing. At the top of the chimney there was a rain damper, held up by four supports so that, though the rain would be turned away, the smoke could escape. McKirk was shooting at the damper. His second shot carried away one of the supports, and one corner of the damper fell across the chimney.

"Tom!" Ned shouted. "The chimney!"

Ned and his two deputies began firing at the top of the chimney. From inside the house half a dozen guns replied. Clouds of birds lifted from the trees, while from the other side of the clearing a deer, startled by the shooting, bounded out of the woods. It ran for several yards before it suddenly realized it was in the open. The animal stopped for a moment, frozen in panic, then turned and bounded quickly back into the cover of the trees.

In less than a dozen shots, Ned and his deputies dropped the damper down onto the top of the chimney. The curl of smoke could no longer escape. The rifles of Ned and his deputies were quiet for a moment while they waited, watching the house.

"Son of a bitch!" someone called from inside the house. Ned could hear a cough, another cough, then a whole chorus of coughs. Smoke started coming through the windows and doors of the house.

"Hold your fire! Hold your fire!" Newsome called from inside the house. "We're a-comin' out!"

"Come ahead!" Ned shouted back. "Get ready," he said to the deputies.

The front door banged open and men, women, and children, coughing and wheezing, ran outside. Two or three of them were waving white cloths over their heads.

"Everyone put your hands up!" Ned called to them. He stepped out of the tree line, holding his rifle in front of him.

"That were a hell of a thang for you to do!" Newsome gruffed. "Cain't you see I got my daughters and their kids in this house?"

"I want Jake Newsome," Ned said.

"I told you, he ain't here," Newsome replied. "Now you go on, get outta here and leave us alone."

"Ned," Beck called to him. "That's Jake Newsome, back near the corner of the house, next to the woman holdin' the baby."

"You sure?"

"He's the fella I seen in the knife fight down to Fort Smith."

The man Beck pointed out was a big man, as tall as old man Newsome and forty pounds heavier. He wasn't wearing a beard, but he did have a handlebar mustache and a shock of raven-black hair. His eyes were dark, and even from this distance Ned could see them flashing fire. He, like the others, had his hands up, but he was wearing a brace of pistols and they were still in the holsters.

"You," Ned called to him. "Shuck out of that gunbelt and come here."

"You got the wrong fella, mister. Jake's my brother," the man said.

"I seen you before, Jake," Beck said. "You got a couple sisters, but I know you ain't got no brother."

"This here's my boy Haskel," the old man said. "Most folks don't know about him . . . he ain't been around these parts too much."

"You come with us anyway," Ned said. "There are enough people in town who know Jake Newsome to prove it one way or another."

Suddenly the man grabbed the woman holding the baby and pulled her to him.

"Jake!" the woman screamed. "What are you

doing?" With her anguished shout the lie was exposed.

"I'm gettin' the hell outta here," Jake growled. "And you're gonna help me."

Ned and his deputies raised their rifles.

"Go ahead and shoot," Jake challenged. "You can't get me without you shoot my sister and her baby too."

"My God, Jake, let the woman go!" Ned called. "She's your own sister!"

"She don't mean nothin' to me, 'ceptin' my way outta here," Jake said. He started easing back toward the tree line on the opposite side of the clearing. By now he had a pistol drawn and was holding it in his right hand, while his left arm was wrapped around his sister's neck, dragging her with him. The baby started to cry.

"Jake, the baby. Let me put down the baby," the woman pleaded.

"Unh-uh," Jake said. He laughed obscenely. "Be glad you got the brat. They want me so bad it might not make no never-mind to them whether you get plugged or not. But they ain't gonna take a chance on shootin' a baby."

"Pa!" the woman screamed. "Pa, make him stop!"

The old man saw at once that Jake was getting away with his ploy.

"You just quit your bellyachin', Sue Ellen," Newsome said. "Ain't neither you nor the baby gonna get hurt none iffen you just take it easy."

Ned and his deputies stood helpless as Jake dragged his sister into the woods, then up the side of a steep hill.

"There's a cave up there," McKirk pointed out.

"That cave ain't gonna do him no good," Beck

said. "I'll flush the son of a bitch outta there if I have to chase him down to the caverns of hell."

Ned and his deputies watched as Jake reached the cave mouth, then disappeared inside. Sue Ellen, free now, started back down the hill.

"Come on!" Ned called, and the three men started toward the cave on the run.

"Are you all right, lassie?" McKirk asked as they passed Sue Ellen on the hillside.

"What do you care? Why don't you just go away? Go away and leave us alone," Sue Ellen snapped.

Beck was the first one to the cave. Knowing that he would make a good target against the light of the opening, he stopped just at the entrance to the cave, then edged in cautiously along the side. Ned and McKirk were right behind him.

"Look, up there!" Ned said. "There's another opening."

"It's a way to the other side of the mountain," Beck said.

The men hurried toward the opening. When they reached it, Beck groaned and pointed toward the valley below. There, riding at a full gallop, was Jake Newsome.

"Damn!" Ned swore.

"Smart lad," McKirk observed. "He had a horse picketed on this side all the time."

"We're five minutes from our horses," Ned said, "and ten minutes getting around to this side. He'll be three miles away by then, but we're goin' after him."

"It ain't gonna be no surprise now," Beck said. "Not for any of 'em."

"What do you mean?"

"Well, Newsome'll tell the others we're comin',"

Beck mused as the three started back down the hill for their own mounts.

"I guess you're right, but I don't care if he tells every outlaw in Arkansas. We're going to bring them back."

McKirk said nothing.

Chapter Seven

Ned and the others held their horses at a steady gallop for more than a mile. Then, because the horses were sweating profusely, they let them walk. The sun had already settled below the tops of the hills, and before long it would be too dark to track.

"At least the son of a bitch'll be eatin' cold tonight," Beck growled. "He won't dare light a fire."

"Aye, laddie, but we'll be doin' no less, and thut's for shurre," McKirk noted.

The next morning they got under way with first light. From the bluff they could see Beaver River, gray and cold under the blankets of mist. As the sun gradually burned away the early-morning fog, the river turned from gray to shining blue. As the day progressed and the sun moved through the sky, the angle of light changed the color of the water from blue to green, and even the leaves and grass looked pale by comparison with the stream's emerald color.

On and on they went, to the peak of one hill, down into the depths of the following hollow, then up to the top of the next bluff, doggedly staying on Newsome's trail. They ate in the saddle and once filled their canteens at a small spring that poured out from a collapsed cave, then sneaked away through mossy boulders. Here, they found trees with blackened trunks where an ancient forest fire had scorched but failed to burn. When McKirk pointed it out Beck said he had seen such things before.

"A lightning strike will start a small fire, but the rain puts it out before it can take hold," he explained.

They tracked Newsome through the rest of that day until the sun set and there was no light left. More anxious men with less experience might have been tempted to go on through the night, but Beck, who was the best tracker of the bunch, knew they could lose the trail and valuable time if they tried. They were frustrated by their failure to find him, but they made camp for the second night.

"I saw a turkey a wee bit ago," McKirk said, stroking his red beard. He took off his black waistcoat, left on his boots. "Wouldn't it be good roastin' on a spit?"

From somewhere close a whippoorwill called.

"I'm that hungry I could even roast a whippoorwill," Beck offered.

"It's bad luck to kill a whippoorwill," Ned said. "Anyway, I don't think they'd be any good."

A horned owl glided by overhead, slipping through the night air in absolute silence as it looked around for its prey.

"Now, there's a creature who'll not be missin' his evenin' meal, dinna ye worry about thut," McKirk said, pointing to the owl.

Ned carved off a piece of jerky and began chewing. "Have we gained on him, Beck?" he asked.

"I think we'll catch up with him by midmorning tomorrow," Beck said. "He pushed his animal too hard yesterday; he's had to rest it today to keep from breaking it down."

"We'll give him a little room, then," Ned said. "I don't want to take him now, until he's led us to the others."

"Do you think the mon will lead us to his friends, knowin' we're on his trail like we are?"

Ned chuckled. "Do you mean am I afraid he'll lead us away to protect his friends? The answer is no. That son of a bitch has no regard for his sister, so I don't think he'd care any more about his friends. No, he'll go straight to them, begging for help. And when he does, we'll be right behind him."

By midmorning the next day the trail was so strong that all three men could follow it quite easily. It was obvious to all of them that Newsome's mount was struggling, because the outlaw had dismounted several times to lead his horse.

"Not too close," Ned cautioned. "I don't want him to realize how near we are. Let's just hold back a bit.

Suddenly the unmistakable sound of traffic reached their ears. They heard a teamster's whistle and the crack of his whip. They heard the heavy rumble of wagon wheels.

"What the hell?" Ned asked. He urged his horse ahead, and the others followed. A moment later they came to a wide, well-traveled road. There were three wagons in sight going west, another heading east. All the wagons were loaded with freight.

"Damn, laddie, I know this road," McKirk said. "I've been down it many a time ridin' shotgun for the Springfield Freight. I dinna realize we was comin' up on it like this. That way lies Harrison."

"About how far?" Ned asked.

McKirk rubbed the bald pate on top of his head and looked around for a moment; then he smiled. "Aboot fi' miles I make it."

They reached the road, and Beck got off and studied Newsome's tracks where they came onto the road. He shook his head.

"Any idea?" Ned asked.

"Iffen I was to bet on it, Ned, I'd say he headed that way," Beck said, pointing south. "But it'd be pure guess. They's so many tracks on this here road —horse, oxen, wagons—they's no way I can be sure."

"If he's going to join up with the others, this is the only way he can go," Ned said. "Come on, let's go to Harrison."

Harrison, Arkansas, was larger than Hollister, Missouri. The town consisted of several streets, crossing at right angles to form blocks. The road they came into town on crossed Main Street, which ran east and west. There was a solid row of well-constructed wooden buildings along Main Street: general stores, leather-goods stores, a couple of laundries, even a library, and a disproportionate number of saloons and gambling halls.

"Let's split up," Ned suggested. "We'll look through all the saloons and gambling halls. Don't forget to check if there are whores working there. A whore's bed might be a good place to hide."

Beck chuckled. "We've ridden the son of a bitch pretty hard if all he can think to do in a whore's bed is hide," he said.

Ned checked four saloons, noticing the sameness of all of them. But then, he decided, they were pretty much alike everywhere. Maybe that was what made them so popular. A man could go into a saloon and feel immediately at home, no matter where he was. Even the songs from the piano sounded the same, and the players might have been the same man in each place, running down the alley from saloon to saloon, just beating Ned to each one.

As Ned came out of the fourth saloon he saw Beck and McKirk. Between them they had checked every other place in town.

"Not a trace of our mon, laddie."

Ned sighed, then pointed toward a restaurant across the street. *Pies made fresh daily,* a sign read.

"If you wouldn't be that opposed to it, we could get something to eat," Ned suggested.

"Now, there's an idea I can sink my teeth into," Beck replied, chuckling at his own joke.

McKirk said nothing but was halfway across the street by the time the other two started.

All three men ordered steak with a side of potatoes. In addition, McKirk ordered half a dozen biscuits and as many eggs. Ned had seen McKirk's appetite before. The Scotsman was tall, but he was thin and angular, and Ned wondered where he put all the food he ate. McKirk was just reaching for the biscuit Ned had left when a woman came into the restaurant and walked over to their table. She looked as if she might have been pretty at one time, though a life of dissipation had robbed her of her looks. Her hair was red... the kind of red that comes from a bottle. There was a bruise under her left eye.

"Are you the marshals?" she asked. "The ones come down from Missouri lookin' for someone?"

"Yes," Ned said. "Jake Newsome. Do you know him?"

"I don't know him," the girl said. "But I know a friend of his. A man named Gerner."

"Gerner's one of the four we're lookin' for," Beck reminded Ned.

"Sit down," Ned offered. He waved his hand toward the waitress. "You want some coffee?"

"If you don't mind my sittin' with you," the woman said. "I might as well tell you... I'm what they call a soiled dove."

Ned smiled. "What do people call you? Soiled, or Dove?"

"What?" the woman asked, not understanding at first. Then she realized he was teasing her and she smiled. The smile did a lot to soften her features, and Ned thought he would like to have seen her a few years ago.

"The folks over at the Peacock, where I work, call me Belle," she said. "My real name's Molly. Molly Butrum."

"Is Gerner in town, Molly?" Ned wanted to know.

"No, not now." Molly put her hand up to her face and touched the bruise, though Ned was sure she wasn't even aware she was doing it.

"He give you that black eye?"

"Yes," Molly said. "Last night." She sighed. "I shoulda knowed better... I seen him around a few times before and I could see he wasn't no gentleman. But he asked me to go upstairs with him last night and, well, I know it ain't none of your problem, but I got me a sick kid and I needed the money for a doctor. I kept waitin' aroun', hopin' someone else would ask me, but Gerner, he made sure nobody else did. Ever' time someone would act like they was goin' to, why, Gerner, he would scare them out of it. Finally the time come I didn't have no choice, so I went upstairs with him. He, uh, likes to get rough with the women he's with, and he give me this... and a few other bruises that I can't show you here."

"How did you know he was a friend of Newsome's?" Ned asked.

"He got real drunk, started tellin' me about some of his friends. One of the names he was sayin' was Jake Newsome. He didn't come right out and say anything they actually done. He said if I really knew he'd have to kill me to keep me quiet. I told him I didn't want to know."

"He and his friends murdered an entire family," Ned said quietly.

"I...I thought it might be something like that," Molly said. She took a drink of her coffee and stared straight ahead for a long moment. "I won't lie to you, Marshal, I've laid with a lot of men...some were pretty good men, some were the scum of the earth. When a man is layin' with a woman, he don't have no secrets. You can look down inside, into his soul, if you know what I mean. When I looked into Gerner's soul I didn't see nothin' but pure evil." She shuddered. "It was like as if I was layin' with Satan hisself. And I don't mean just 'cause he beat me. I been beat up before." She shook her head as if trying to get him out of her mind. "Anyway," she went on, "when I heard you three was checkin' with all the girls to find Newsome, I figured I'd come over and tell you about Gerner. Maybe if you knew where Gerner was, you could find Newsome."

"Do you know where Gerner is right now?"

"I can't swear to it, Marshal, but I can make a pretty good guess."

"How so?"

"The bartender told me Gerner tried to cash in a house token."

"A house token? What's that?"

"It's like money, only it can only be used at the place that sells 'em. You can use it for everything from drinks and a meal to paying one of the girls for her services. They don't none of the places use tokens here in Harrison. Fact is, the only place I know around here that does use 'em is the Paradise Saloon, and that's down in Jasper."

Ned wiped his mouth with the napkin by his plate, then stood up and looked at his two deputies.

"Gents," he said, "we're going to Jasper."

Chapter Eight

Down the creek road toward Jasper Ned Remington led his two deputies, trotting his horse sometimes, other times urging it into an easy, ground-eating lope. If Molly was right, if Newsome had joined up with Gerner, then there was also a chance that all four men were together now.

On the one hand, that was good. He was out to bring them all in if he could. On the other hand, all four of them united could make a formidable challenge. He knew they were all dead shots; he knew they had been in dozens of gunfights, both during the war and in the brushes with the law they had had since the war.

Jake Newsome climbed onto a rock from which he could see the road for three miles back. Beyond that point the road curved around behind a range of peaks.

"See anything?" Gerner asked. Gerner, a short, hairy man with gray eyes and a pug nose, took the last swallow from a whiskey bottle, then tossed it against a nearby rock. The bottle broke into two pieces.

"Goddammit, Gerner, what for'd you break that bottle?" Ephraim Flatt asked. Flatt was tall and gaunt, with sunken cheeks and bad teeth. "We coulda got us five cents for it back in Jasper."

"Five cents." Bill Kimmons snorted. "You worried about a nickel now, are you?" Kimmons was between Gerner and the others in size. He was clean-shaven and had gray eyes. His most distinguishing feature was his left hand. There were only three fingers on his left hand, the result of a badly fused mine during the war.

"It's worth a beer," Flatt insisted.

"Iffen we'da robbed that bank up in Hollister liken I wanted to, we wouldn't be worryin' 'bout no nickel for a beer."

"You see anythin' yet?" Gerner asked again.

"No."

"You don't see nothin' 'cause they ain't comin'," Gerner said.

Newsome stroked his mustache. "They're a-comin'," he said. "I've had them on my trail for three days now. I can feel it in my gut when they're close, and they're close now."

Gerner walked over to his horse and slipped his rifle out of the saddle holster. He worked the lever.

"What are you fixin' to do?" Kimmons asked.

"If they really are comin' like he says, the best thang we could do is lie here and wait for 'em."

Flatt giggled. "Yeah," he said. He pulled out his

rifle. "Yeah, we can just wait right here, ambush 'em soon as they come into range."

The other two got their own rifles. Newsome took the horses back into the woods a short distance, then tied them down. He came back, saw that his three partners were already getting into position in the rocks. He checked the load in his rifle, eased the hammer back to half cock, then hunkered down behind a rock and waited.

"Let them come on up to no more'n a couple hundred yards," Gerner said. "We got all the advantage. They don't have no idea we're here."

"Shhh!" Newsome said. "There they are! I told you they was comin'."

Three riders came into view at the most distant point the road was visible. They were riding at a brisk pace, coming on unsuspectingly.

"Be patient," Gerner said quietly. "Remember what I said. Just be patient."

On the riders came, to a mile, half a mile, a quarter mile. Gerner raised his rifle and rested it carefully against the rock. "Just a little closer," he said. "A little closer before we fire."

Newsome shifted position to get a better aim. As he did so he dislodged a loose stone, and the stone rolled down the hill, right into the largest, unbroken piece of the whiskey bottle. The stone shattered the glass and it made a loud, tinkling noise.

"Goddammit!" Gerner shouted angrily. "We're in for it now!" He raised up and fired his first shot.

The sound of the crashing bottle reached Ned's ears at about the same time Gerner suddenly reared up. Ned could see that the man was holding a rifle pointed toward them.

"Ambush!" he shouted, pulling his pistol at the same time. He snapped off a shot, knowing he was out of range, hoping only to make the bushwhacker hurry his own shot. The ploy worked: Gerner fired quickly, then dropped down behind the rock.

Beck and McKirk were off their own horses nearly as quickly as Ned. All three slipped their rifles from the saddle sheaths and ran, low, toward the rocks to the side of the road. Beck threw a handful of dirt toward the horses, shooing them out of the line of fire.

"Looks like we found 'em," Beck observed dryly.

"Aye, thut we did."

"If we can make it to the creekbed, we can work our way up closer without coming under their fire," Ned said.

"We're right behind you, Marshal," Beck replied.

The three men stood up and ran, crouched over, toward the creekbed. Four rifles spit bullets toward them, but the ambushers were more than four hundred yards away and they were shooting downhill at moving targets. None of the bullets came close enough even to kick up dirt around them.

"Newsome, you dumb son of a bitch!" Gerner swore. "Iffen you hadn't kicked that rock down we woulda had 'em by now."

"Where are they?" Newsome asked, sticking his head cautiously over the rock and looking down toward where the targets had been. "Where are they? I can't see 'em."

"They headed for the crickbed," Kimmons said. "I seen 'em go in there."

"Where at does that crick come out?" Flatt asked anxiously. "Is there any way they can get the drop on us?"

"No way," Kimmons said easily. "The crick curves away, right down there. That's as close as they can get."

No sooner were the words out of Kimmons's mouth than was there a puff of smoke and the bark of a rifle from a clump of bushes at exactly the place Kimmons was pointing out. The bullet hit the rock right in front of them, then hummed off, but not before shaving a sliver of rock to kick up into Kimmons's face.

"Ow! I been hit, I been hit!" Kimmons called, slapping his hand to his face. "I been shot right in the jaw!"

Flatt looked up at him and laughed.

"You ain't been hit," he said. "That ain't nothin' no more'n a piece of rock."

Two more bullets hit the rocks then and chips of stone flew past the men.

"I don't like this!" Gerner said. "They're gettin' too damn close." He fired a couple of shots toward the bush just below the puff of gunsmoke.

"Hey, Newsome, look down there. Ain't that their horses comin' back up the road?"

"Yeah," Newsome said. He raised his rifle and pointed toward the animals. "Shoot the horses. They can't come after us if they ain't got no horses."

All four men started shooting at the three horses. The horses had wandered much closer than Ned and his deputies had, but they were still a couple of hundred yards away and they were still downhill. As a result none of the animals was hit, though this time the bullets were close enough to strike the ground nearby. Frightened by the bullets hitting so close to them, the horses turned and ran in a group off the road, but parallel to it, toward the shelter of a large bluff a quarter mile away.

"Dammit! We missed!"

"No matter, it'll be an hour or so before they can round those critters up again," Newsome said. "Let's get the hell out of here while we got a chance."

The four outlaws started for their own horses, snapping off shots toward the brush as they ran.

With his rifle, Ned followed them, firing at the man in the lead. The man went down, but the other three made it to their horses. They kicked their horses into motion and in just a few seconds were behind a rocky ledge, out of the line of fire. One down and three to go.

"Don't leave me, you bastards!" the one on the ground shouted. "Don't leave me!"

Ned and Beck started toward the outlaw on the ground, holding their weapons pointed toward him.

"I'll get the horses," McKirk offered.

The outlaw sat up, saw them coming, and threw up his hands. "Don't shoot, don't shoot," he pleaded. "I'm hurt. I'm hurt bad."

"Which one are you?" Ned asked when he reached the wounded outlaw.

"Gerner. Tom Gerner," the man said. "You got to get me to the doctor. I seen men get wounds no worse'n this durin' the war, and when they wasn't treated fast enough, why, they'd wind up losin' a leg."

"You'll hang as good with one leg as you will with two," Beck said.

Ned put his rifle down, then knelt beside Gerner. He cut the trouser leg away with his knife and saw the ugly black hole where the rifle bullet had gone into the flesh. The bullet had come out the other side. There was a goodly amount of blood, but it wasn't pumping as it would be if an artery had been hit. And there didn't appear to be any shattered bone. He ripped up some more of Gerner's trouser leg and used it to make a bandage, tying it in place with strips of cloth.

"You could hang with one leg," Ned said. "But you probably won't have to. You're not hurt bad."

"The hell I ain't. What do you know? You ain't the one with the bullet in you."

"No, but I'm the one that put the bullet in you," Ned said as he tied off the last strip. "And if I had wanted to hurt you bad I would have done it. I promised Judge Barnstall I'd bring the four of you back to meet his justice, and that's just what I intend to do."

McKirk came up then, riding his horse and leading the other two.

"Horses all right?" Ned asked.

"A wee nervous, but nae a scratch," McKirk said.

Beck brought Gerner's horse over and held it while Gerner climbed into the saddle.

"Where you takin' me?" he asked.

"Into Jasper," Ned said. "I'm going to leave you in jail there until I round up the other three."

"Jasper's my territory, mister," Gerner said. "You don't expect no Arky lawman is going to put me in jail on the say-so of somebody from Missouri, do you?"

"The badge I'm wearin' ain't Missouri," Ned said. "It's U.S. And that means it's good in every state, territory, and in the Nations. Your Arkansas lawman damn well better lock you up, or I'll throw his ass in jail with you."

Chapter Nine

As Ned and his deputies rode into Jasper with their prisoner, someone on the street pointed to Gerner. "Hey!" he shouted. He ran down the sidewalk, his footfalls sounding loudly on the boards. "Hey, the law's got Tom Gerner. They're bringin' in Tom Gerner!"

"What?"

From both sides of the street people began appearing, and they walked quietly along the lawmen's path, watching with wide, curious eyes.

Ned stopped his group in front of the sheriff's office. "Get down," he said to Gerner.

"Who are you, mister?" someone from the crowd called. "You got no right to bring one of ourn in like this."

"They ain't even got me a doctor," Gerner complained. "Look here, I got a ball in my leg, an' they ain't even got me a doctor."

"I said get down," Ned repeated. McKirk reached up and took Gerner by the back of his collar, then pulled the prisoner down. Gerner winced as his feet hit the ground.

"You can't treat me like this," Gerner complained.

The door to the sheriff's office opened and a tall, thin, white-headed man stepped out.

"What's goin' on here?" the sheriff asked.

"Howdy, Ben," Ned said, recognizing the sheriff. "Boys, this here is Ben Mason. We've rode together some in the past."

"Ned Remington," Ben said. "It's been a long time." He saw the star. "And a U.S. marshal? How's the wife and child? You got a girl, don't you?"

Beck and McKirk looked at Ned warily. They didn't know how he'd react to someone bringing up this painful subject.

"Yeah," Ned said without elaboration. "I got a girl. Get inside, Gerner."

The five men went inside. Beck and McKirk stayed by the front window, looking out over the street. The crowd had evidently gathered more out of curiosity than anything else, for they dispersed quickly once the excitement was over.

"What happened, Ben?" Ned asked. "How'd you let this town get away from you like this? You used to be a pretty good lawman."

Sheriff Mason looked down toward the floor in shame. "I got older, slower," he said. "I took a slug in my shoulder up in St. Joe. Another one in my gut in Omaha. I figured to come down here, find me some small town where roustin' drunks would be the worst of it. Only I found myself right in the middle of the wildest bunch I ever laid eyes on. And to make things worse, I arrest 'em and Judge Binder lets 'em go. I...I'm ashamed to say, I decided to roust the drunks and let the others alone."

"Binder's not the judge anymore," Ned said. "Barnstall is."

"Barnstall? Samuel Parkhurst Barnstall?"

"The same."

Sheriff Mason smiled. "Barnstall will set them straight," he said. The smile left his face. "But it's too late for me. I don't have any respect...if I started now, I'd get run out of town on a rail."

"I'm not going to tell you how to run your town, Ben," Ned said. He looked over at Gerner. "But I am going to tell you how to keep my prisoner. I want him here when I get back."

"He will be," Ben promised. "Hey, tell me about Barnstall. Has he made a dent yet?"

"I reckon," Ned answered. "He hung three men just the other day."

"Who'd he hang?"

"Amos Cullimore, Lou Woods, and Bill Sisley."

"Knew 'em all three," Ben said. "Can't think of a better thing to have happen to 'em. Come on, Gerner. Back to the cell with you."

"What about a doctor?" Gerner asked. "This here leg is hurtin' me somethin' awful. You gotta get me a doctor in here. It's a law that you gotta take care of your prisoners."

"I been lawin' a long time, and I ain't never heared of no law like that," Mason answered. "Have you?" he asked Ned. He was smiling broadly.

"Don't think I have," Ned agreed.

"What? You can't leave me back here like this. My leg'll get gangrene an' it'll have to come off!"

"Well, I think there is a law that says we can take off a leg if we need to," the sheriff went on. "If it gets that bad, we'll do somethin' about it, don't worry." Mason put Gerner in a cell and closed the door; then he and Ned walked back to the front of the jail, leaving Gerner behind, cursing in fear and anger. After the door between the office and cells was shut, the sheriff spoke again.

"I'll get Doc Swinney to come down here and take a look at it. I've seen worse. I think he just wants to yell a bit. So Barnstall is takin' hold pretty good, is he?"

"Yeah."

Mason rubbed his chin for a moment, then went over to his desk and opened the drawer. He pulled out a few wanted posters and looked at them. "These are all federal posters," he said. "Maybe I'll see what I can do about drummin' up a few customers for your new boss."

"I'm sure he'd like the business," Ned said. "By the way, where's a good place to eat?"

Mason thought for a moment; then he smiled. "Why don't you go over to the Bull's Head? That's about as good a place as any. It's a saloon, but they'll cook you up a steak or pork chops, some taters, and black-eyed peas."

"Sounds good enough to me," Ned replied. He nodded to his two deputies, and the three men took their leave of the sheriff's office while Mason shuffled through the wanted posters he had pulled from his drawer.

A sign outside the saloon promised cool beer, and Ned thought that would go pretty well with his meal. He pushed his way through the batwing doors, and the other two followed him inside. It was so dark that he had to stand there for a moment or two until his eyes adjusted to the interior. This was one of the nicer saloons he had been in for a while. The bar was made of burnished mahogany, with a highly polished brass footrail. Crisp, clean white towels hung from hooks on the customers' side of the bar, spaced every four feet. A mirror was behind the bar, flanked on each side by a small statue of a nude woman set back in a special niche. A row of whiskey bottles sat in front of the mirror, reflected in the glass so that the row of bottles seemed to be two deep.

Even the bartender seemed to be a part of the decor, with slicked-back black hair and a handlebar mustache. He stood behind the bar, industriously polishing glasses.

"Is the beer really cool?" Ned asked.

The bartender looked up at him, but he didn't stop polishing the glasses.

"It's cooler than spit," he said matter-of-factly.

"I'll have one."

"You gentlemen?"

Beck ordered a beer also, while McKirk ordered his usual scotch.

The bartender set the drinks in front of them. Ned picked his up, then turned and looked around the place. A card game was going on in the corner, and he watched it for a few moments while he drank his beer. Suddenly the back door opened and Sheriff Ben Mason came in. He pointed a gun toward the table.

"Arnold Presley? I've got paper on you down at the office. I've come to take you in."

"You gone crazy, Sheriff?" One of the cardplayers said. "You got no right to bust in here on our card game like this."

"I have every right," the sheriff said. "I've got a

wanted poster on you in my office, and a gun in my hand. What more do I need?" The sheriff looked over at Ned and his deputies, and Ned realized then why the sheriff had sent them over here. He wanted their backing when he made his arrest.

Beck started to pull his pistol, but Ned put his hand out to stop him.

"Ain't we gonna help him?" Beck wanted to know. "If he has papers, and we're sworn officers of the law, it's our duty to help."

"We'll be more help by staying out of it," Ned said. "If we jump in now, what's going to happen to Ben after we're gone? Let's let him play it out."

"Come on, Presley. Let's go," the sheriff said.

Three of the four cardplayers got up slowly from the table and moved back out of the way. The fourth player, the man Ned figured to be Arnold Presley, remained seated. His hands were still on the table in front of him, still holding the cards.

"Aw, now, Sheriff, you done went 'n' busted up a winnin' hand," Presley grumbled.

"Money won't be doin' you any good where you're goin'," the sheriff said. "Stand up and face me; then, with your left hand, unbuckle your gunbelt, slow 'n' easy."

Presley stood up and turned to face the sheriff. For a moment it looked as if he had a notion to try him.

"I'd advise you not to try anythin' foolish," the sheriff said. "Give yourself up peaceful 'n' you'll at least get your day in court."

"Whose court? Judge Binder's court? You know he'll let me go, Sheriff. He did the last time, he'll do it again."

Sheriff Mason grinned. "Binder ain't the judge no more. They got a new man...a man named Barnstall. Some of your friends have already run into Judge Barnstall. You remember Cullimore, don't you? And Sisley and Woods?"

"Yeah, I know 'em. They're pretty good boys."

"Was pretty good boys," the sheriff replied. "Barnstall hung 'em. Ever' one of 'em."

Presley's face blanched. "What are you talkin' about, Sheriff? You plannin' on sendin' me up before a hangin' judge?"

"That's about the size of it," the sheriff said. "Now shuck out of that gunbelt."

Ned was watching the drama unfolding before him when he heard a sound, a soft squeaking sound as if weight were being put down on a loose board. He looked up to the top of the stairs and saw a man standing there, aiming a shotgun at the back of the sheriff.

"Ben, look out!" Ned shouted. When he shouted his warning, the man wielding the shotgun turned it toward Ned.

"You squealin' son of a bitch!" he shouted. The shotgun boomed loudly.

Ned had no choice then. He dropped his beer and pulled his pistol, firing just as the man at the top of the stairs squeezed his own trigger. Ned and the others had jumped away from the bar as the shotgun fired, and it was a good thing, because the heavy charge of buckshot tore a large hole in the top and side of the bar right where the three men had been standing. Some of the shot hit the whiskey bottles and the mirror behind the bar, and pieces of glass flew everywhere. The mirror fell except for a few, jagged shards that hung in place where the mirror had been, reflecting twisting images of the dramatic scene before it.

Ned's shot had been more accurately placed, and the man with the shotgun dropped his weapon and grabbed his neck. He stood there, stupidly, for a moment, clutching his neck as blood spilled between his fingers. Then his eyes rolled up in his head and he fell, twisting around so that, on his back, headfirst, he slid down the stairs, following his clattering shotgun. He lay motionless on the bottom step with open but sightless eyes staring up toward the ceiling.

The sound of the two gunshots had riveted everyone's attention on that exchange, and while their attention was diverted from him Presley took the opportunity to go for his own gun. The bar was suddenly filled with the roar of another handgun as Presley shot at Sheriff Mason.

The sheriff had made the mistake of looking at the man Ned shot, and it was nearly his last mistake. Fortunately for the sheriff, Presley's aim wasn't as good as Ned's had been, and the .44-caliber ball from his gun whistled through the crown of the sheriff's hat, whipping it off his head but doing nothing more.

Sheriff Mason recovered quickly from his moment of distraction and whirled back toward Presley, returning his fire. The sheriff's bullet struck Presley in the forehead, and the impact of it knocked Presley back on a nearby table. He lay belly-up on the table with his head hanging down on the far side, while blood poured from the hole in his forehead to form a puddle below him. His gun fell from his lifeless hand and clattered to the floor. Sheriff Mason swung his pistol toward the three men who had been playing cards with Presley, thumbing back the hammer as he did so.

"Any of you men aimin' to take a hand in this?" he asked gruffly.

"Not me, Sheriff," one of the men said, throwing up his arms.

"No, not me, either," a second one shouted. He, like the other two men, threw up his hands.

Gunsmoke from the four charges had merged to form a large, acrid-bitter cloud that drifted slowly toward the door. Beams of sunlight became visible as they stabbed through the cloud. Ned heard rapid footfalls on a wood walk outside; then several people stepped in through the swinging doors, drawn by the excitement. They looked at the two bodies on the ground, then at the sheriff, who still had his gun drawn. No one said a word; they just looked at him in shock. This wasn't the sheriff they had known.

"I wanna thank you, Marshall," Sheriff Mason said. "Thank you for stayin' out while you could... and for comin' in when you did. And for remindin' me of my duty," he added.

"Glad to be of service," Ned replied.

"Don't worry none about your prisoner," the sheriff went on. "He'll be here when you get back. Sam," he added, speaking to the bartender.

"Yes, Sheriff," Sam answered. Ned noticed there was a newfound respect in the bartender's voice.

"Whatever these fellas eat or drink is on the county. I'll take care of the tab."

"In thut case, laddie, I'll be havin' a wee bit o' steak to be goin' with the pork chops I already ordered," McKirk said.

Chapter Ten

Ned and McKirk were sitting in the sheriff's office drinking coffee when Beck came back from the livery stable. He had taken Gerner's horse down to be boarded, paying for it by giving the liveryman a chit that could be exchanged in federal court for money.

"I looked through Gerner's saddlebags," he said. "I found this here piece of paper... thought you might make somethin' out of it."

Ned took the paper from Beck and looked at it for a moment.

"It's a receipt for a pair of boots," he said. "Bought at the Boots and Saddles shop in Tahlequah."

"Tahlequah? That's out in the Nations," Beck said. "I thought these yahoos lived here in Arkansas."

"Maybe they have a place out there too. People in

their line of work often have more than one place to go."

"Whatta you think?" Mason asked. "Are the three of you going on to Tahlequah?"

"Maybe. Tell me, Ben, does the train go all the way to Tahlequah? I saw track laid when I come through there a few days back."

"Yep, not a reg'lar run, but they been carryin' people and stock back and forth," Ben said. "Ain't hooked up to Fort Smith yet, but track'll take you to Tahlequah anyways."

"Have ye a plan in mind, laddie?"

"Yes," Ned said. "John Angus, you and I are going to put our horses on the stockcar and take the train to Tahlequah. Tom, you're the best tracker of the three of us; I want you to stay here, then start toward Tahlequah on horseback. When McKirk and I get there we'll look around, see if they have a place there, then start back on horse to join up with you. If we get lucky, we'll trap them between us."

Ned Remington sat looking out the window of the train as the terrain rolled by. He didn't really like riding a train; he found it too boring. Horseback was the way to travel...on horse you were part of the world. In a train you just sat quietly while the world passed you by.

In Huntsville, a young man wearing an ivory-handled pistol, leather chaps, and highly polished silver rowels got on the train. Like a strutting peacock, he swaggered back and forth through the car a few times, but Ned paid little attention to him. In Springdale a very pretty young woman boarded the train. As she boarded she smiled shyly at Ned. There was something about her that reminded him of his Katy, and he felt a tug at his heart as he thought of his daughter, sitting in a stupor, back in the convent. The pain had been reactivated when Sheriff Mason asked about her. That happened often when he would run into old friends, friends he had not seen in a long time, who didn't know about his tragedy. He hadn't yet found an easy way to handle that.

The peacock evidently knew the girl. He called her by name—Lucinda—and he moved to sit near her. Ned put them and his own heartache out of his mind and began to think of the promise he had made to Judge Barnstall to bring his prisoners back within a week. That already seemed unlikely. He hated to fail at anything, even a self-imposed deadline. He might not get them as quickly as he thought he would, but he would get them. He was certain of that.

"Tahlequah! We're comin' into Tahlequah, folks," the conductor said, walking quickly through the car. Ned had been dozing, and McKirk nudged him.

"What? What is it?"

"I would let ye sleep on, laddie, but the conductor says we're coming to Tahlequah. We'd be wantin' to get our horses now."

"Yeah, you're right," Ned said, stretching. "Conductor, how far are we?"

"Just a mite under two miles, sir," the conductor answered.

"Thanks."

"Go ahead, I'll join ye. I'll just get a wee drink of water first."

Ned got up and walked forward toward the stockcar while McKirk headed for the water scuttle at the rear of the car. When Ned stepped out onto the vestibule he saw the girl and the peacock standing on the platform between cars.

"Please," the girl was saying. "Please, just leave me alone."

"Come on, I seen the way you was lookin' at me at the dance last week. You ain't foolin' no one by playin' hard to get."

Ned had already put his hand on the door to go into the next car when he heard the exchange, and he stopped and looked back at them. He was reluctant to interfere in any discussion between a man and a woman because he knew that playing reluctant was often part of a woman's courting ritual. In this case, however, the expression on the young lady's face and the tone of her voice told him that she wasn't playing a game. She was serious when she told the peacock she didn't want to be bothered.

"Mister, why don't you be a good boy? Go on back in the car and leave the lady alone," Ned said.

The peacock looked toward Ned as if shocked that anyone would butt in.

"What did you say to me, old man?"

"I told you to go on back into the car and leave the lady alone."

"Why don't you just go to hell?" the peacock said menacingly. He turned back to the girl as if dismissing Ned, but Ned wouldn't be dismissed. He stepped across the gap between the two cars, then grabbed the peacock by the scruff of the neck and the seat of his pants.

"Hey, what the..." the peacock shouted, but whatever the fourth word was going to be was lost in the rattle of cars and his own surprised scream as Ned threw him bodily off the train. The peacock hit on the downslope of the track base, then bounced and rolled through the rocks and scrub weed alongside the train. Ned leaned out far enough to see him stand and shake his fist, but by then the train had swept on away from him.

"He'll be all right," Ned said. "He'll have a little walk into town, is all."

The girl laughed and even above the sound of the train he could hear the musical lilt of her laughter. God, what he would give to hear Katy laugh like that!

"What is it?" McKirk asked, stepping onto the platform then. "What happened?"

"The fella with the silver just got off the train," Ned said. He looked at the girl. "I hope I wasn't out of line, miss. I hope you were serious when you told him you wanted him to leave you alone. I mean, you did seem to know him. At least, I heard him call you by name. It's Lucinda, isn't it?"

"Yes, Lucinda Gray. My father owns a hotel in Tahlequah, that's why I know him. His name is Jack Kimmons, and he comes to the dances at the hotel on Saturday nights. I know him, but believe me, he is no friend of mine."

"Kimmons, is it? Gurl, did you say his last name be Kimmons?" McKirk asked.

"Yes," Lucinda said. She looked at the two men curiously. "Why? Does that name mean something to you?"

"As a matter of fact, it does," Ned said. "Bill Kimmons is one of the men we're looking for. Do you know him?"

"I know of him," Lucinda said. "Bill Kimmons is Jack's older brother. I've never seen him at any of the hotel dances, and for that I am very glad. Why are you looking for him?"

"He got into some trouble back in Missouri," Ned said.

"Oh, you're both marshals," Lucinda said, noticing their badges for the first time.

"Yes. Do you know where we might find Bill Kimmons?"

"I don't know where they live. You might try the Bucket of Blood. It's a saloon. You can't miss it, it's painted blood-red. That's where the real bad men are, most of the time."

"Bucket of Blood?" Ned's eyebrows knitted. That was one he had missed when he passed through with Switcher. It was just as well. It was illegal to sell whiskey in the Nations. He'd have to tell Barnstall about it.

The train started slowing down.

"Excuse me," Lucinda said. "I must get off here. I want to thank you again for coming to my rescue, but please, be careful. People like Bill Kimmons and his friends don't have much regard for the law."

"Thanks for your concern," Ned said. "And the information."

Ned and McKirk didn't have to ask directions. From the moment they took their horses off the train they could see the Bucket of Blood. It sat, like a ripe tomato, at the far end of Tahlequah's main street. No more than a minute later they were tying their horses to a hitching rail in front of the place.

"Come on, Angus," said Ned, "we're going to break the law. This saloon's on the wrong side of the border."

The bartender drew a mug and set it, with foaming head, in front of Ned. He put a shot glass of scotch in front of the tall man with the red beard. Ned slid ten cents' worth of silver across the counter, then drank the first one down without taking away the mug. He wiped the foam away from his lips and slid the empty mug toward the bartender.

"That was for thirst," he said. "This one's for taste."

With the second beer in his hand, Ned turned his back to the bar and looked out over the saloon. Unlike the elegant saloon back in Jasper, this one was fairly new, having only recently graduated from a tent. The bar and the plank floors still smelled of fresh wood. There were half a dozen tables scattered about; a card game was in progress at one of them, while the others held only drinkers and conversationalists. A bar girl sidled up to them. She was heavily painted and showed the wear of her profession. There was no humor or life left in her eyes, and when she saw that neither Ned nor McKirk appeared to show interest in her, she turned and walked back to the table she had come from.

The piano player wore a small, round derby hat and kept his sleeves up with garter belts. He was pounding out a rendition of "Buffalo Gals," though the music was practically lost amidst the noise of two dozen conversations. Ned was on his third beer when the batwing doors swung open and Jack Kimmons came in. He had scratches and bruises on his face, and his clothes were dirty and torn.

"Jack! What the hell happened to you?" someone asked.

"Some son of a bitch pushed me off the train," Jack said.

Everyone in the saloon laughed.

"Goddammit! It isn't funny!" Jack said. "I was just standin' there on the vestibule, mindin' my own business, when he sneaked up behind me and shoved me off."

"You weren't minding your own business," Ned said. "You were making unwanted advances toward a young woman."

Ned's voice cut above the laughter and the buzz of the saloon, and it suddenly grew very quiet. Jack looked toward the bar and saw Ned.

"You!" he said in a choked voice. "You're the one did this to me! Pull your gun, you bastard! I'm going to shoot your eyes out!"

There was a quick scrape of chairs and tables as everyone scrambled to get out of the way. Only McKirk didn't move away from Ned. McKirk looked over at the bartender, who had ducked down behind the bar.

"Bartender, would ye be for pourring me anither scotch?" McKirk asked in a calm voice.

"Mister, are you crazy?" the bartender hissed. "Get out of the line of fire!"

With eyes of ice, McKirk looked back toward Jack Kimmons, who was standing in the doorway with his arm crooked, his hand hovering just above his pistol.

"Are ye talkin' aboot the mon in the doorway there?"

"Yes, for God's sake."

"Oh, dinna fret none aboot thut. I'm not in the line of fire. As soon as that lad over there twitches, Ned'll put 'im down. Nae, this is the safest spot in the room." Several people gasped at McKirk's calm words.

"Would ye be pourrin' my scotch now?"

The bartender raised up just far enough to hand McKirk the bottle.

"Thanks," McKirk said. Calmly he poured a glass, then looked toward Jack, still standing in the doorway. Jack, like the others, had heard McKirk's calm declaration, and now he was hesitating. His hand was shaking visibly.

"Are ye still there, laddie?" McKirk asked. He took a swallow of his scotch, then wiped the back of his hand across his mouth. "If I were ye, I would nae stay aroun'. Aye, look at ye, now. Sure, and ye got the shakes so bad Ned here's likely to make a mistake. He's likely to think you're goin' for your gun, when really all you're doin' is peein' your pants."

Several in the saloon laughed.

Jack opened and closed his fingers several times; then, quickly, he turned and hurried back through the doors. His retreat was greeted with the laughter of everyone in the saloon.

"Step up to the bar, boys," someone shouted joyfully. "The drinks are on the house. Any time I can see either one of the Kimmons boys backed down like that, it's worth a round."

"Beer!" "Whiskey!" two dozen voices called as everyone in the place hurried to the bar.

The man who had bought the drinks came down to stand beside Ned and McKirk.

"What brings you fellas to Tahlequah?"

"A federal warrant," Ned said easily.

"A federal warrant? What the hell are you talking about. What..." Suddenly the man stopped and licked his lips. He saw the badges Ned and McKirk were wearing. "You're the law," he said.

"We are."

"If I'da knowed that, I'da never bought a round of drinks." He turned to leave, but Ned put his hand on his shoulder and stopped him.

"That's not very sociable," he said.

"Ain't my intention to be sociable. You aimin' to close this place down?"

"Never mind about that. Where can we find Bill Kimmons and his friends?"

"You just braced down his brother. Wait around— maybe he'll find you."

"I don't want to wait. Where can I find him?"

"I don't talk to the law."

"Hell, tell 'em, George," somebody else said. "We don't owe none of them bastards out there nothin', that's for sure."

"You want 'em to know, you tell 'em," George said.

"The Kimmons got 'em a shack about a mile west of town. But you better be warned, they don't live out there by theirselves. They got three more live with 'em. Fellas by the name of Newsome, Flatt, and Gerner."

"Gerner's not there anymore," Ned replied. "We left him in jail back in Jasper."

"And now you're goin' after the others?"

"That's right."

"You two are either the bravest men I ever saw ... or the stupidest. I don't know which."

Chapter Eleven

Beck trailed the outlaws all day long, staying just agonizingly out of sight. He was close enough to them that the horse droppings were still moist, but he never got close enough to see them. Ned was right —they were headed straight for Tahlequah. If they kept going in the same direction and at the same speed, they'd be caught in the pinch between Beck and his two partners within another few days.

That is, if they kept going the way they were. It had been Beck's experience that men on the run seldom went anywhere in a straight line. That was why he was always very careful at every opportunity they had to leave the trail to make certain they hadn't.

Just before nightfall Beck rode onto a high bluff, then, dismounting, looked west toward the setting sun. Sometimes in the red light of sunset, trail dust from the horses would give off a glow that could be seen for many miles. That was what Beck was looking for. He didn't see any glowing dust, but way in the distance he did see a curving glint of the railroad. From this point to the section of the railroad he was looking at was probably fifteen to twenty miles. Fifteen to twenty miles of rugged hills and gullies, rocks and creeks, tangled undergrowth and thick trees. Skilled woodsmen who knew the territory could hide in these Ozark mountain forests for thirty years if they wanted to and the best tracker in the world couldn't find them. Beck knew that the men he was trailing were skilled woodsmen... and they knew the territory. But it never crossed his mind that he might not find them. He would find them, no matter how long it took.

Beck turned away from his observation point. Below him, on the other side of the rim, was the Buffalo Fork River. He didn't have to go see it, he could hear it. He had been following it most of the day and would probably trail along beside it for at least two more days. He walked back to his Indian pony and untied his bedroll. This was as good a place as any to spend the night.

Early morning.

The bluff rose beside the river like a huge black slab against the velvet texture of the sky. Overhead, the stars spread their diamond glitter across the heavens, while far in the east a tiny bar of pearl-gray light gave the first indication of impending dawn.

The wind, which had moaned and whistled across the hills and through the hollows all night long, was quiet now, and a predawn stillness had descended over the land. The only sound to be heard was the rippling flow of the water, perhaps fifty feet below.

Beck, who had camped on top of a bluff overlooking the Buffalo Fork River, picked up his bedroll and tied it behind the cantle. He opened one of the saddlebags and took out his old blue pot and a little sack of coffee he had bought in Jasper. He ran the crook of his arm across his lower jaw and felt a growing stubble of beard.

"Damned if I ain't gonna give the Scotsman a run for his money on growin' a beard," he said aloud. He preferred to be clean-shaven, but when he was on the trail it was easier to let it go than to lather up and shave.

Beck got a fire going, then measured out a careful amount of the coffee. A moment later the air was permeated by the rich aroma of the brew. As he waited for it he looked over at his horse, standing quietly where it had spent the night. So well trained was his Indian pony that Beck never bothered to stake him out. He knew he would be there in the morning.

"All right, horse, you tell me. Are we doin' the right thing, or are the bastards gonna slip away?" With Ned and McKirk coming back from Tahlequah, he was sure they would catch up with the outlaws, unless they were a lot better than he thought.

The horse blew, and pawed at the ground.

"Yeah," Beck said, grinning. He poured himself a cup of coffee. "That's about what I thought you'd say."

The coals from his campfire glowed cherry red in the predawn darkness, and Beck threw some more wood on to enjoy its warmth. It had been cold and damp on the ground last night, and it would be another couple of hours until the sun was high enough to push away the morning chill.

Suddenly, and for no discernible reason, Beck realized that he wasn't alone. The hackles rose on the back of his neck, and he stiffened.

"Come on in," Beck said as calmly as he could.

He heard a chuckle. "I figured we couldn't get this close without you'd know we was here. Anyhow, we seen your fire, 'n' smelt your coffee, 'n' figured you'd be up to sharin' a bit," a voice called from the dark.

"Which one do you be?" Beck asked.

"I reckon we've met before. I'm Jake Newsome."

Beck cursed himself for not being more alert. He had been so deeply lost in thought a few moments earlier that his quarry had been able to approach this close without being seen or heard. He had suddenly gone from the hunter to the hunted.

Beck looked over toward his horse. His gunbelt was draped across the saddle. He had not yet put on his guns this morning, so his best bet was to do nothing that would arouse the suspicions of his visitors. He held his arms out so they could see he was making no attempt to go for a gun.

"Newsome, Flatt, Kimmons, come on in." Beck pointed to the coffeepot suspended over the dancing flames of his fire. "There's plenty of coffee here."

Beck turned to search the darkness for the intruders, but he saw nothing at first. Then he heard the sound of someone walking, and finally the three men emerged from the darkness into the golden bubble of light put out by the fire. All three were holding guns.

"You been sticking on our trail like stink on shit," Newsome said. "I don't mind tellin' you, we're gettin' damn tired of it."

"Where are your friends?" Kimmons added.

"They're around," Beck answered.

"Yeah, well, too bad we can't say that about our friend, ain't it? Where is he? Is he dead?"

"You'd be talkin' about Gerner?"

"That's right."

"I 'spect he is dead," Beck lied. They might have the drop on him, but there was no way they were going to get any information out of him.

"Did you kill 'im?" Flatt asked.

"I might have. I tried hard enough."

"Tom Gerner were my cousin," Flatt said. "He were my blood. I don't take too kindly to folks killin' my kin."

Newsome poured himself a cup of coffee, then took a drink, slurping it through his extended lips to cool it.

"You done stepped on your dick, ain't you, lawman?" Kimmons said, pouring himself some coffee, using a little tin cup he produced from his pocket.

"What do you mean?"

"Lettin' yourself get caught by the folks you was tryin' to catch. It's kinda like the rabbit catchin' the fox, ain't it? Only we ain't rabbits, an' you damn sure ain't no fox."

"You was right, Bill," Newsome said. "You said you thought they was only one a-followin' us right now, an' sure 'nough, here he is, all alone. One of him an' three of us. Now, ain't that a good piece of luck for us?"

"You ain't played out your hand yet," Beck said. "You might not be as lucky as you think."

Newsome laughed. "Oh yeah, I think we are. Tell 'im, Flatt. Tell 'im what we're gonna do."

Flatt smiled broadly, showing broken, crooked, and stained teeth. "Well, now, what we're aimin' to do is just shoot you 'n' take what you got. Your food, your bedroll, your saddle, your horse. We'll sell it . . . make maybe sixty, seventy dollars out of the deal. You'll be dead 'n' out of our hair, and we'll pick up a little money. That makes us come out the winner. What do you think of that?"

Beck looked toward his horse and pistols, perhaps ten yards away. Kimmons chuckled.

"You may be fast as greased lightnin', Deputy, but them hoglegs o' yourn is nigh thirty foot away and they's three of us. You ain't never gonna get to 'em. You really ought to be more careful when you're trailin' men like us. We're smarter'n your average outlaw."

"Yeah." Flatt chuckled. "Smarter'n the average outlaw."

"Can I say good-bye to my horse?"

Newsome chuckled. "Good-bye to his horse. You get that? He wants to get over there by them guns. Go ahead, Deputy, try it. You might make it."

Beck looked long and hard at his pistols while the three outlaws chuckled at his predicament. Suddenly he made a feint toward his horse, then surprised them by jumping the other way. The three outlaws had been anticipating Beck's move toward his guns, so they fired in that direction. Their guns flashed bright orange in the dim morning. It was twenty yards through the dark toward the edge of the bluff, and Beck headed for it on a dead run.

"The son of a bitch went the other way!" Newsome shouted in frustration, and the outlaws' three guns roared again, this time in Beck's direction. Beck felt a sharp, stabbing pain and knew that one of the balls had caught him in the hip. He reached the edge of the cliff, then launched himself into the maw of darkness.

"Where'd he go? Where'd the son of a bitch go?"

Beck felt himself falling through black space, down, down, toward the water below. He hadn't looked at the surface of the river last night. He didn't know if he was plummeting toward a bloody and painful death on rocky cascades or the safety of a deep pool. He knew the chances were fifty-fifty it could be either one. He thought a quick prayer.

Beck hit the water, then went under. It was so cold that it took his breath away... but, mercifully, there were no rocks. He had fallen cleanly. He felt a burning pain where the bullet had hit him, and he wondered how badly he had been hurt.

Newsome, Flatt, and Kimmons were standing on the edge of the bluff, firing down into the blackness below. The great orange flame patterns of their pistols were lighting up the trees around them. Burnt powder and acrid smoke drifted up into their faces. After about three shots apiece, Newsome started yelling at the others to quit firing.

"We ain't doin' nothin' but wastin' bullets," he said. "We can't even see down there."

"How far down is that, do you reckon?" Kimmons asked.

"Who the hell knows? It could be two or three hunnert feet."

Flatt giggled insanely. "I bet he's dead. I bet he's flatter'n a pancake down there on them rocks."

"Throw a rock over," Kimmons suggested.

"Why would I want to do a damn-fool thing like that?" Newsome asked.

"You can tell how deep a hole is that way," Kimmons said. He picked up a rock and tossed it over. It was a relatively small rock and they never heard it hit.

"Whooee!" Flatt said. "That rock ain't hit yet! That son of a bitch is dead!"

Newsome put his pistol back in his holster. "Get his horse and let's go," he said.

The three men turned away from the edge of the bluff; then Kimmons let out a shout of anger.

"Goddam!" he said. "The horse! The goddam horse is gone!"

"Gone! Where could he have gone?"

"He musta run away when we started shootin'," Kimmons said.

"Damn. That son of a bitch was so dumb he didn't even tie up his goddam horse," Flatt said.

Beck let himself be carried about a mile downriver before he decided to come out. On at least three occasions the river ran into rapids and he was swept painfully across the rocks. By now he had so many cuts, bruises, and hurts that he wasn't even sure which hurt was the bullet wound.

Beck worked his way toward the riverbank, then grabbed an overhanging limb. Slowly, painfully, he pulled himself out of the water, then crawled until he was on a relatively flat piece of ground. He fell on his back, exhausted from his effort and shaking with cold. The frigid water did have one beneficial effect, however. The pain of his cuts, bruises, and bullet wound was held in check by the numbing cold. Beck closed his eyes and either went to sleep or passed out.

* * *

Beck felt something poking his face. He turned his head, hoping it would go away, but the nudge returned. Finally the insistent nudging penetrated the fog of his brain and he gradually began to return to consciousness. He opened his eyes and saw his pony standing over him, poking at him with his nose. His gunbelt still hung from the pommel, his rifle still in its sheath. The sun was high and his clothes were nearly dry. He was beginning to get warmer. On the negative side, he could feel the pain of his injuries, especially the bullet wound.

"All right, horse, I'm awake," Beck finally said. He sat up, then lowered his pants to find the wound. The bullet had cut a groove in his hip, taking out flesh at a place where he had very little flesh to give. It looked exactly as if someone had taken a spike and scraped him about half an inch deep. It was painful and ugly, but at least there was no ball to remove. He looked around, found some moss, and made himself a poultice.

Chapter Twelve

The stagecoach trip from Springfield to Galena was not for the faint of heart. Passengers had to hang on as the driver whipped the horses over roads so narrow that the inside wheel hubs would be scraping mud and moss while the outside wheels were pushing pebbles over the edge to fall hundreds of feet. Sometimes the cutbacks were so sharp that to the passengers it appeared as if the team were going in the opposite direction.

There were four passengers on the stage: an overweight, balding drummer who kept a cigar in his mouth for the entire trip, lighting a new one when the old one grew too small; a young woman going to Galena to teach school; an older woman who was the schoolteacher's aunt; and Judge Barnstall.

Judge Barnstall made the trip quite often and had learned a method of bracing himself against the lurches and lunges of the coach. The drummer had traveled enough that he, too, was pretty adept at shielding himself from the more violent blows of the stage, but the two women were having a very difficult time. Barnstall suggested that the women should separate, one of them sit by him and the other sit by the drummer. That way the men's bodies could absorb some of the blows, sparing the ladies much of the punishment.

"I don't know if that would be proper," the schoolteacher said. "Perhaps we had best stay just as we are."

Less than a mile and at least ten violent lurches later, the schoolteacher's aunt stood up.

"I don't know about you, dear, but, proper or not, I'm going to take the kind gentleman's suggestion."

Barnstall smiled as the old lady changed seats with him. A few moments later even the teacher was ready to admit that it had been a good move.

"What kind of place is Galena?" the teacher asked.

Judge Barnstall started to answer, but the drummer answered first.

"I can tell you what kind of place it is," he said. "It's a place of evil and perdition. It's a place where a judge has gone rampant. Why, just last week they hung three men right in the middle of town."

"You mean there was a lynching?" the teacher asked, horrified.

"No'm, it warn't no lynchin'. It was a hangin' done by the new hangin' judge they got down there, a fella by the name of Barnstall."

Barnstall looked at the drummer.

"Do you know this judge?" Barnstall asked.

"I ain't never seen 'im yet. This here's my first time into Galena since he took over from Lucius

Binder. Ah, Judge Binder, now, there was a good man. A good man. He hardly ever found it necessary to hang someone."

"Perhaps these three men should have been hanged," the teacher suggested. "If you have never met Judge Barnstall, you should at least give him the benefit of believing he's a just man. After all, he is a judge, and he should be presumed to be worthy of the position unless he proves himself to be otherwise."

"Believe me, miss, I know his kind," the drummer said. "He's the kind that takes the law into his own hands. He's got the power of the rope behind him, an' he's gonna run things his way, come hell or high water."

"Young man," the teacher's aunt said, "you'll forgive an old woman for speaking out like this, but I don't think you have the slightest idea what you're talking about."

"Why, what do you mean, madam?" the drummer asked.

"In the first place," the old lady said, "if he's the judge, he has every right to take the law into his own hands. That's what he is paid to do. And in the second place, if there really is evil and perdition in this country, then perhaps a little stern application of the law is just what's needed. I for one am glad for a judge like this man Barnstall."

"What do you think of it, sir?" the teacher asked, smiling prettily at Barnstall.

Barnstall cleared his throat. "Well, I don't know if I ought to comment, ma'am," he said. "I'm afraid I'd be a little prejudiced."

"Why so?" the drummer asked.

"Because, sir," Barnstall said, fixing the drummer

with a steely gaze, "I *am* Judge Samuel Parkhurst Barnstall."

The drummer, who had just lit a cigar, bit it in two. The old lady had a very difficult time swallowing a laugh.

Deputy Jim Early was waiting for the judge when he stepped down from the coach at its stop in front of the Galena Hotel.

"Any news?" Barnstall asked.

"A wire from Jasper. They've caught Tom Gerner, have him in jail there."

"What about the other three?"

"They got away," Jim said.

"Damn. I would've sworn Marshal Remington would have them back by now. I was counting on it."

"Don't worry, Judge. There aren't three better men in the country for the job you've sent them out to do. They'll bring 'em back, all right; you can make book on that."

"Are they still in Jasper?"

"I doubt it. The wire said that Ned and McKirk were going by train to Tahlequah. Beck was going to follow on horseback. They figured to catch the other three in between."

"I suppose that's as good a way as any," Barnstall said. He ran his hand through his hair. "I want those bastards, Jim. I want them standing before my bench so I can look straight into their eyes and damn their souls to eternal hell."

"It'll happen, Judge. Believe me, it'll happen."

"Where's the boy?"

Jim smiled. "You mean our new law officer? Like as not he's with Hammer or Norling. He's got it in his mind he's gonna be one of your deputies. He's got a badge and a gun—"

"A gun? The boy's only ten years old."

Jim chuckled. "It's not anything he can get hurt with. It's an old Slocum thirty-two revolver. The kind they used to sell on the back pages of *Harper's Weekly*. It won't work now—hell, they damn near didn't work when they were new."

Jedediah came running around the corner then. When he saw the judge he stopped running and approached with as much dignity as he could manage.

"Did Deputy Early tell you? I'm going to be a deputy too."

"I'm sure you'll make a fine one," Barnstall said.

The boy's face clouded over. "The only thing, who ever heard of a deputy in St. Louis? That's where I'll be when I go to live with Aunt Louise."

"Why, boy, St. Louis has more policemen than all the law officers in the rest of the state," Jim told him.

The boy's face brightened. "Really? Hey, maybe I'll be a policeman instead of a deputy."

"You'll be a good one, I'm sure," Judge Barnstall said, rubbing the boy's hair.

"And the first thing I'm going to do is testify against the men that...that..." The brave facade nearly slipped away as Jedediah recalled what he had witnessed. Tears slid from his eyes, and he took a deep breath.

"I know it's going to be hard, Jedediah," Barnstall said quietly. "But you can do it."

"No, sir," Jedediah said defiantly. "It ain't gonna be hard at all. I'm goin' to testify; then I'm goin' to stand right out here and watch 'em hang. Ever' one of 'em. I just wish I was big enough to bring 'em in for you."

"Son, we've got people who can bring them in," Barnstall said. "But we've only got one man who can testify against them."

"You mean me, don't you?" Jedediah said. His face lit up in a broad smile. "When you said one man, you were talkin' about me."

"Yes, sir, I guess I was," Barnstall said. "You had to grow up quick, but I reckon you're a man now."

"You're not too much of a man to eat a licorice whip with me, are you?" Jim asked. "I was down to the store while ago, saw they'd put out a fresh jar."

"I . . . I reckon I could eat one with you," Jedediah said, trying to keep the smile off his face.

Judge Barnstall watched Jim Early and his young cousin walk down to the store; then he crossed the street to the courthouse and went upstairs to his office. Because of his trip to Springfield, he had no cases to try until tomorrow. Now would be a good time for a quiet brandy.

A few moments later, Barnstall held the snifter under his nose and thought about the territorial jurisdiction he had established and the deputies Ned Remington had gathered to ride for him.

In addition to Ned, Tom Beck, John Angus McKirk, and Jim Early, there were others, just as deadly and just as effective. Men like Frank Shaw, a man with so many bullet holes in him he seemed damn near immortal to those who went up against him. Bucky Kermit was a true loner who went into the Nations as though born there. He always got his man . . . dead or alive. There were Jedediah's two friends, Kurt Hammer, a German who had shortened his name from Hammerschmidt, and Dan Norling, a

Swede. From somewhere, Ned had even found a Negro, a man named Jimson Weede, who claimed to be descended from African royalty. No one could look the powerful black man in the face and tell him otherwise. The last man Ned had collected to ride for him was Faro, a man with no past and a single name. No one knew anything about Faro and no one wanted to try and find out.

Barnstall was new, but he had assembled a law-enforcement team that would stamp his name on the entire territory. He knew they would roam wherever they had to go, tame towns, settle scores, hunt down criminals. They were men who lived by the gun and for the gun. The Colt was their God, and the Henry rifle their long suit in the deadliest game of all.

Samuel Parkhurst Barnstall would always be the man behind them. When his deputies served one of his warrants Barnstall wanted the fugitive's blood to turn chill. And the fugitives he most wanted now were the ones who had murdered his uncle and his uncle's family.

"This is one thing I'll have to learn, I guess," he said quietly. "I'll have to learn patience. Jim's right. Ned will bring them in."

The sound of a pistol shot rolled down the mountainside, picked up resonance, then echoed back from the neighboring mountains. A young man holding a smoking pistol turned and looked at his audience of four with a smile on his face. He had just broken a tossed whiskey bottle with his marksmanship.

"I'd like to see any of you do that," he said.

"Yeah, Jack, that was pretty good," one of the others, a man named Brewster, agreed. "But breakin' bottles ain't the same thing as standin' up to someone. Like the fella in the Bucket of Blood yesterday."

"They's a difference between bein' brave an' bein' a fool," Jack Kimmons said. "They was at least two of 'em in the saloon. Who knows how many others they was? Don't you worry none. If I ever get a chance to go up agin that marshal face to face, just him an' me, I'll kill him."

One of the other men guffawed. "You're just mad 'cause that purty little girl in town won't have nothin' to do with you."

Jack pulled his gun and rested the barrel on the upper lip of the man who was laughing. "Well, now, Athens," he said, slowly cocking his gun. The cylinder turned with a metallic click. "Maybe we'll just see what kind of luck you have with girls when you ain't got no nose."

Brewster raised his arm and a small pistol popped into his hand from its concealed position up his sleeve. He put the small gun to Jack's temple.

"Now put your gun away, Jack," Brewster said quietly.

Jack laughed. "Haw! Whatta you think you're goin' to do to me with that little pepperbox?"

"Put a little bullet in your little brain," Brewster answered.

Jack held his pistol on Athens for a moment longer. "I could kill him before you pulled the trigger," he warned.

"I don't care all that much about him anyway," Brewster said. "But if you drop that hammer on him, I'm going to kill you."

"Back off, both of you," one of the others said. "Jack, how do you think your brother's gonna feel if he gets here and finds out we been killin' each other off? You think he's gonna let us go on that bank job with him and the others?"

Jack waited a moment longer, then eased the hammer down on his gun. "Sure," he said, smiling. "I didn't mean nothin' by it anyway."

Athens let out a sigh of relief, then wiped the sweat off his forehead. He smiled nervously.

"Where the hell are they anyway? I thought they were supposed to get back to Tahlequah last night."

"Maybe they run into a little trouble," Brewster said. "That marshal you had the run-in with yesterday come out to the place lookin' for 'em. If they're lookin' for 'em here, they're most likely lookin' for 'em all over."

"Yeah? Well, if they are in trouble we're gonna have to get them out of it," Jack said. "Bill said he knew where there was a bank with a lot of money in it, and I aim to get my hands on some."

"Maybe we ought to go look for 'em," Brewster suggested.

"We'll give 'em a few more days," Athens said.

Chapter Thirteen

Ned Remington and John Angus McKirk began to backtrack from Tahlequah. The area was rugged and thick-wooded, cut eons ago by the mountain springs and rivers. There was a maze of gullies and crevices, small canyons and deep cuts, any one of which could provide the three outlaws with a way to leave the trail.

Had they not been on the trail of desperate and dangerous men, the journey would have been quiet and restful, with its many trees and abundant supply of water. Here and there, though, thick underbrush camouflaged hidden caves and niches, perfect places for outlaws to hide. As a result, there was no relaxing of the vigil as the two lawmen made their way back to rejoin their partner.

"John Angus, I have a feeling we're going to hear again from that bunch around Tahlequah," Ned said, speaking not only of Jack Kimmons, but also of

Brewster, Athens, and the others they had learned about.

"Aye, Marshal, they're as scurvy a lot as ye ever hope to find, tha's for sartin. It would nae surprise me if they try an' join up with the bla'-guards we're trailin'."

"I hope Tom Beck has picked up their trail. We sure have nothin' to show for our efforts."

"Aye. Except the notion to be on the lookout for their friends when we do catch 'em," McKirk added.

Tom Beck spent three days in the same place, resting and trying to recover from the bullet wound in his hip. The first day wasn't so bad; he had slipped in and out of consciousness most of the day. He got a fever the second day and feared the wound might get infected. On the third day the hip was still so painful that it was difficult to walk or ride, but the fever was gone and the pus was draining. This was the fourth day and, though the wound was sore, he knew now that there was no longer any danger from infection. Tomorrow he would start for Tahlequah to try and cut the outlaws' trail again, or at least to meet Ned and McKirk.

When Beck went down to the water to clean the wound and apply a new poultice, he saw two riders in the distance. By the way they were sitting their horses he knew right away that it was Ned and McKirk. He pulled his pistol and fired three times, waited a few seconds, then fired three more times. He smiled when he saw them urge their horses toward him.

* * *

"You've no idea what happened to them after that?" Ned asked after listening to Beck's story of his early-morning escape.

"No," Beck answered. "I was going to start after them again tomorrow. I don't reckon you cut their trail coming back?"

"No. They've given us the slip, temporarily."

"Aye," McKirk said. "The laddies are makin' a wide circle, and we're taggin' along like sheep-dogs."

"So what do you think, Tom? You're the bloodhound."

"Jasper," Beck said. "I don't think they believed my story about us killin' Gerner. They get to town, they'll hear the news quick enough. They'll want to break their friend out of jail."

"Aye, they may at that," McKirk agreed. "If they think they killed the laddie here, they'll be thinkin' they can pull Gerner out of jail with nae trouble."

Ned smiled. "All right, let's go into town and wait for them. Are you up to riding, Tom Beck?"

"Well, you ain't gonna leave me here, that's for damn sure," Beck said. He stood up and walked around, testing his mobility. "They ain't nothin' left but a little soreness. I'll be just fine. Hell, take one leg away and I can still beat any one of them sons of bitches in a ass-kickin' contest."

Ned laughed. "You ask me, I think we ought to put you and Gerner in a closed room...see who comes out. What do you think, John Angus?"

"Aye," McKirk answered with a barely perceptible smile. " 'Twould be somethin' to see, tha's for sartin."

* * *

The animals were spattered with mud and ragged with travel as Newsome, Kimmons, and Flatt rode onto the single street of Deer, Arkansas, and trotted past the line of false-fronted business establishments crowding the splintered wooden walk.

The three men, slumped in their saddles, tired from the false trails they had been leaving, made careful inventory of the buildings: a pool hall, a small restaurant, a leather-goods shop, a church, and a saloon. They pulled up in front of the saloon and went in, moving straight to the back of the room, positioning themselves so they could see everyone who came in.

"What for did we come here?" Flatt asked. "I hate this town. I've always hated this town."

" 'Cause they ain't likely to thank of comin' down here," Kimmons answered. "By now they've learnt from Gerner that we got us a place over in Tahlequah."

"If he's still alive, you mean," Newsome said. "Don't forget, that deputy we jumped said he was dead."

"He mighta just been sayin' that to throw us off," Kimmons said. "We gotta figure Gerner has told 'em about our place."

"Gerner ain't gonna talk none," Flatt insisted. "If he's alive."

"We need to find out whether he's dead or not," Kimmons said. "Let's split up, move aroun' town, an' ask a few questions. We can meet back here in an hour, then decide what to do."

"All right," Newsome agreed. He stood up. "But be careful. Remington coulda crossed us up. Him and that red-bearded fella with him could be down here, just layin' for us."

One hour later the three outlaws returned to the same table. They had all three learned the same thing, but Flatt was the one who spoke.

"He ain't dead, he's in jail in Jasper. He was shot in the leg, but it ain't bad. We can get him out."

"Let's not be so hasty," Newsome put in.

"Iffen it was you in that jail you'd want us to get you out," Flatt insisted.

"Ephraim's right," Bill Kimmons said. "Besides, if we get Gerner out of jail we can go back to Tahlequah and pick up my brother and his friends, then empty that bank up to Hollister. They ain't nobody, not even the whole town, could stand up to nine of us. It'll be like durin' the war when we rode with Quantrill and ol' Bloody Bill. Why, we could take that bank as easy as pie."

"There ain't no bank easy as pie," Newsome said.

"The one at Hollister is. We done shot down the constable there, an' we kilt one of Barnstall's deputies besides. They ain't no one left except Remington and the Scotsman, and we got them wanderin' aroun' who knows where, lost as little puppy dogs. They ain't nobody in this town seen hide nor hair of 'em."

Ephraim Flatt laughed. "That's for sure," he said. "That's for dang sure. Come on, Jake, let's get Gerner out and go get that bank like Kimmons said."

"We do that, that new hangin' judge they got up to Galena is gonna send ever' one of his deputies after us."

"Let 'im. We'll have enough money we can get clear outta the territory," Kimmons said. "We can go anywhere we want. Hell, we can go to California if we want to."

"Yeah," Flatt said excitedly. "We can go to California and spend our poke. Hey, Bill, how much money you reckon that bank's got?"

"I reckon nine or ten thousand dollars, anyway," Kimmons replied.

"Oooweee. Nine or ten thousand dollars...let's see, if we brung in them five others"—Flatt held up his hands and counted his fingers—"that'd make nine of us. We'd get...uh...how much would we get?"

"I don't know, exactly. More'n any of us has ever seen, that's for sure."

"We'd get more iffen we didn't worry 'bout gettin' Gerner outta jail," Newsome suggested.

"We gotta get him out," Flatt said.

"Why do we gotta?"

"You know why. 'Cause he's my cousin...he's kin."

"All right, all right," Newsome agreed. "If we're gonna do it, let's do it and be done with it."

"It ain't gonna be hard," Flatt insisted. "The sheriff they got in Jasper's an old man. All he ever worries 'bout is drunks."

"Then you do it," Newsome suggested.

"Me? Alone?"

"You said yourself they weren't nothin' to it," Newsome taunted. "If that's right, then just go on in and get 'im out."

"All right, I'll do it," Flatt vowed.

"You better get a extry horse," Kimmons suggested. "Get a extra horse for 'im, 'cause like as not the sheriff'll have his put away somewhere."

"I reckon you're right," Flatt agreed.

* * *

Up in Jasper, Ned and McKirk could hear the music of the band from halfway down the street. Ned hummed along with the music as his boots trod loudly on the boardwalk. "It's a pretty tune," he said.

"Aye, 'tis a lilting air, I'll agree," McKirk said. "Though 'twould sound better on the pipes."

"Those infernal things would run everyone off," Ned said.

"Ha' ye nae ear for music, then, laddie?"

They were waiting for what they were sure would be an attempt to rescue Tom Gerner. Beck, still favoring his wound some, was in the jail watching Gerner. Ned and McKirk had been patrolling the town all day. It was Saturday night, and there was a dance in the Morning Star Hotel. The music had drawn the two lawmen to the hotel, to be sure, but they also knew that the crowd of dancers would be a good place for the outlaws to hide until they were ready to make their move.

McKirk tipped his hat to the wife of one of the townspeople as the couple approached the hotel; then, gallantly, he held the door open for them.

Inside, the lights glowed, the music played, and men and women laughed and whirled about on the dance floor. Ned and McKirk stood just inside the door for a moment, looking out over the sea of girls in butterfly-bright calico and men in denim and homespun. Ned saw one particularly pretty young girl, and in his mind's eye the girl became his daughter. Katy... surrounded by half a dozen admirers. Katy... wearing a light blue dress, embroidered with beads of many colors. Katy... standing tall and beautiful, attracting men to her like bees to a flower.

REMINGTON

The music stopped and one of the musicians lifted a megaphone.

"Ladies and gents! Choose up yur squares!" he called.

The pretty young girl—Katy, in Ned's mind—was chosen and the squares were formed. The music began, with the fiddlers loud and clear, the guitars carrying the rhythm, the accordian providing the counterpoint, and the Dobro ringing out over everything. The caller began to shout. He laughed and clapped his hands and stomped his feet and danced around on the platform in compliance with his own calls, bowing and whirling as if he had a girl and were in one of the squares himself. The dancers moved and swirled to the caller's commands.

"I've looked at ever' face in here, laddie, and they are nae here," McKirk said.

With McKirk's words, the spell was broken. It was no longer Katy; it was just another pretty girl at another Saturday dance. His Katy was back in Missouri, trapped in her own private hell. Ned sighed.

"All right, let's go back out on the street," Ned said. "You go up Main, I'll go down First."

"Aye," McKirk agreed.

In the darkness, two hundred yards away from the last building on Main Street, three men stood looking toward the soft lights of the town. Out here the sound of the band was barely audible. They heard a woman's scream, not of fear, obviously, because it was followed by her laugh which carried clearly above everything else. Overhead, a sudden blaze of gold zipped across the sky.

"Oh, shit," Flatt said. "A fallin' star. That means bad luck."

"Yeah, well, just make sure it's bad luck for someone else," Newsome said. "Now, you know what to do?"

"Yeah. I'm gonna walk in real slow, leadin' the two horses so's no one notices me. Then I'm goin' into the sheriff's office, and if he's there I'll lock 'im in his own jail and get Gerner out."

"Don't do no shootin'. Half the county's at that dance. One shot would bring them down on you like ducks on a june bug," Kimmons cautioned.

"Don't worry. I know what I'm doin'," Flatt insisted.

Newsome and Kimmons stood in the darkness and watched as Flatt, leading the two horses, walked slowly down toward the town.

"That boy ain't got sense enough to pour piss out of a boot with the directions written on the heel," Newsome said.

Kimmons laughed. "Seein' as how they ain't none of us can read, I don't know what good the directions would do any of us anyhow."

"What we ought to do is just leave," Newsome said. "Leave him and his cousin in there."

"We ain't leavin' 'em," Kimmons said.

McKirk heard them before he saw them. There was the unmistakable sound of at least two horses, walking slowly, quietly, down the street. He was curious why anyone would try to keep their animals so quiet when the rest of the town was a cacophony of sound.

McKirk stepped in between the general store and the newspaper office. Back in the shadow between the two buildings, dressed in his black trousers and waistcoat, he completely slipped from the view of anyone who might be on the street. He watched until the two horses were even with him; then he saw that the man leading the horses was Ephraim Flatt. He looked around quickly, making certain that the others weren't with Flatt. When he saw that Flatt was alone, he stepped out into the street with a pistol in each hand. He didn't even have to speak. All he had to do was cock the weapons. The cold, metallic sound of the turning cylinders spoke for him.

Flatt dropped the reins and stuck both arms straight in the air.

"I knowed it," he said. "Soon as I seen me that fallin' star, I knowed it was gonna be bad luck."

Chapter Fourteen

The night creatures serenaded each other as Newsome and Kimmons waited outside Jasper. A cloud passed over the moon, then moved on, bathing the little town in dull silver. The dance had ended some time ago and now the band was quiet, though someone was playing a piano and its ringing sound could be heard out here, a counterpoint to the melody of the whippoorwills and owls. It had been almost two hours since Flatt went in to get Gerner.

"Where the shit is he?" Newsome asked, pacing around nervously in the darkness. "He said it was going to be so easy. Why ain't he back?"

"We're gonna have to go in after 'im," Kimmons said.

"To hell with 'im. To hell with Flatt an' his cousin."

"We're goin' in after 'im," Kimmons insisted.

"All right, all right, we'll do what you say," Newsome gave in. "But if anythin' goes wrong, it's your fault."

Ned's head slipped forward and he jerked it back, realizing he had just dozed off. He looked over at McKirk, and McKirk's chin was down on his chest, a rhythmic breathing indicating that he was asleep.

"Scottie, wake up," Ned said.

McKirk raised his head, then stroked his beard and let a long sigh of air escape from his lips.

"Aye, laddie, 'tis not human to go as long with nae sleep as we have."

"We'll sleep in the morning," Ned promised. "I don't want to miss it if the other two decide to come in."

"Dinna ye worry none," McKirk said. "If they come in, we'll be ready."

Ned and McKirk were in the shadows between two buildings, positioned right across the alley from the back of the jail. Flatt and Gerner were in the same cell, and their window opened onto this alley.

Since Tom Beck and Sheriff Mason were in the front of the jail, Ned didn't think the outlaws would try to go through that way. If there were going to be an attempt made tonight, it would be made back here. When the attempt came, Ned would be ready.

They sat quietly for several more moments; then McKirk spoke.

"Lad, I seen the way ye was lookin' at the young lass at the dance tonight."

"Did you, now?" Ned asked.

"Aye. And I know what ye was thinkin'. Ye was thinkin' o' your own sweet dotter an' wonderin' why it couldn't be her there, 'stead o' the pretty young lass that was."

Ned was shocked that McKirk was so perceptive. He hadn't spoken a word; how was McKirk able to to guess so accurately what he had been thinking?

"I suppose you're right," Ned said in a gruff voice. "Such thoughts often trouble me."

"Dinna fret yoursel' so much about Katy. The Lord will nae give the lass more to bear than she can handle. I'm thinkin' there's a peace in her heart that, like the prayer book in the old church says, passeth all understandin'."

"Maybe you're right," Ned agreed. He was touched by McKirk's sympathy.

"Aye. An' maybe I talk too much," said the man who spoke so little.

The two men were quiet for several more moments; then they heard a quiet, shuffling noise somewhere down the alley. Ned put his hand on McKirk's arm, and both were instantly alert.

Ned and McKirk stared down the alley until they saw shadows moving within the darkness. A moment later the shadows materialized into Bill Kimmons and Jake Newsome. The two outlaws moved to the jail window.

"Ephraim!" Kimmons called out in a loud stage whisper. "Ephraim, Tom! You two in there?"

"Bill, is that you?" Flatt's voice replied. "I knowed you'd come for us. I knowed you would."

"Hang on, we'll have you out in a jiffy," Kimmons called back.

Ned and McKirk crossed the alley then and were no more than five feet away when Newsome turned.

"Bill, it's them!" he warned.

Kimmons whirled around with his hand in front of him. Ned saw the soft, dull gleam of a knife blade.

"It's a little Arkansas toothpick for you, my

friend," Kimmons said, smiling evilly. Kimmons was crouched a little, right arm out, blade projecting from across the upturned palm between the thumb and index finger, with the point moving back and forth slowly and hypnotically. Kimmons danced in and raised his left hand toward Ned's face to mask his action. He feinted with his right, the knife hand, outside Ned's left arm as if he were going to go in over it. In the same movement, when Ned automatically raised his left arm to block, Kimmons brought his knife hand back down so fast it was a blur, and he went in under Ned's arm.

The knife seared Ned's flesh like a branding iron along his ribs and opened a long gash in the tight ridges of muscle. The cut began to spill blood down his side, and Ned could feel it pooling at his belt. Out of the corner of his eye, Ned could see that McKirk and Newsome were also engaged in a fierce struggle.

Ned brought his left hand down sharply, almost by reflex, and knocked away the knife Kimmons was now holding with an air of careless confidence. He heard the knife clatter against the side of the building. Now they were even...hand to hand...except Ned was cut and Kimmons wasn't.

Kimmons put his hands up to protect himself, but Ned saw a quick opening that allowed him to send a long left to Kimmons's nose. Ned felt the nose go under his hand and he knew he had broken it. The nose started bleeding, and in the light that spilled from the window of the jail Ned could see the blood running across Kimmons's teeth. It was a terrible-looking sight, but Kimmons continued to grin wickedly, seemingly unperturbed by his injury.

With the cut across his ribs, Ned wasn't as flexible as he normally was. The exertion was painful, and he was having to favor his side. As a result, Kimmons seemed to be holding his own in the fight. Ned kept trying to hit the nose again, but he was unable to connect.

Though Kimmons had sustained the one blow to his nose, he now began to think he was winning the fight. He started swinging wildly, believing that if he could connect with just one blow he could put Ned out.

After four or five such swinging blows, Ned noticed that Kimmons was leaving a slight opening for a good right punch, if he could just slip it in across his shoulder. On Kimmons's next swing, Ned timed it perfectly. He threw a solid right, straight at the place where he thought Kimmons's nose would be. He hit the nose perfectly and had the satisfaction of hearing a bellow of pain from Kimmons. It was an effective and bruising punch, but it cost Ned; he felt his side open up and winced as sharp pain shot through him. Steeling himself against the agony in his side, he threw a whistling left into Kimmons's stomach and, when Kimmons dropped his hands, followed up with a right to the chin, dropping Kimmons like a sack of flour.

Ned turned to see how McKirk was doing with Newsome, just in time to see McKirk throw a hard left to Newsome's Adam's apple. Newsome choked, then fell to his knees. McKirk followed that with a roundhouse right to the jaw, and Newsome fell across Kimmons, both men lying unconscious in the dirt behind the jail.

REMINGTON

* * *

"Maybe I ought to follow you three men around," Dr. Swinney suggested. "I could make a living just patching you up."

Ned, McKirk, and Beck were in Sheriff Ben Mason's office. Ned and McKirk had their shirts off. Ned had a bandage wrapped all the way around his waist; McKirk had a bandage on his arm.

"Both you men will be carrying scars from this one."

"What about our four prisoners, Doc?" Ned asked. "Any reason why they can't make the trip back to Missouri?"

Dr. Swinney chuckled. "I know you probably don't like hearing this, being as you boys won the fight. But they're in better shape than you are." Swinney looked over at Tom Beck. "All three of you, considering the wound in your hip."

"My hip feels fine, Doc, honest," Beck said.

"I'm sure it does, and it's healing very well. You did a good job treating yourself out there. I couldn't have done better if I had been there. But it's a pretty tough ride back to where you're going, and all three of you have been injured. I'm just saying take it easy, that's all. Don't do anything that might open the wounds up again."

"Nothin' to it now, Doc," Ned replied. "We got the ones we come after. We're just gonna take 'em home."

"Marshal, you want me to ride as far as the border with you?" Sheriff Mason offered. "Just in case some of their friends try somethin'?"

Ned smiled. A week ago Sheriff Mason had been barely willing to let them lodge Gerner in his jail. Since that time he had gained some self-respect.

Jasper was going to be a better place for its citizens to live in now.

"Thanks, Ben, but we'll make it just fine," he said. He smiled again. "If the county's got another meal in the kitty, I will let you buy my deputies and me one last breakfast before we start out."

"Come on, I'll eat with you," Mason said. "I know just the place."

Breakfast consisted of fried eggs, biscuits, gravy, salt pork, a side of potatoes, strawberry preserves, and coffee. McKirk wasn't the only one to eat hearty. Not only was the food exceptionally good, Ned and the others realized they were about to go on the trail again. Since they had no intention of stopping to hunt, jerky and water would be their fare for most of the time.

There was an added treat to the breakfast. It was served by the same pretty young girl Ned had watched at the dance the night before. Sheriff Mason informed Ned that the girl's father had died of dropsy two years ago and she and her mother had survived by turning their house into a restaurant.

"More coffee, Marshal?" the girl asked sweetly, bringing the coffeepot over to the table, holding it with a pot holder against the heat.

"Yes, thank you," Ned said.

"Marshal, this is Miss Amy Matthews. Amy, these are U.S. marshals from Judge Barnstall's court. Marshals Remington, McKirk, and Beck."

"I'm pleased to meet you," Amy said shyly.

"I've a daughter about your age," Ned said. "You remind me of her."

"Please tell her I said hello," Amy said.

"Yes, I'll do that," Ned said. He had surprised

nimself by speaking of Katy like that. Most of the time she was a painful side to his life that he preferred to keep hidden. But he found comfort in speaking of her with this girl, and he was glad that he wasn't jealous of the girl's ability to enjoy life.

"Ah, ladies," McKirk said as the girl returned to the kitchen, "if God made anythin' nicer to look at than a purrty lass, he saved it for his own self," McKirk said.

"If you think the girl is pretty, you should see her mother," Mason said.

"Well, now," Ned teased. "Are you showing an interest in the girl's mother?"

"No, not really."

"Why not? You said she was a widow, didn't you?"

"I...I...by God, I don't know why not," Mason said, smiling broadly. "Maybe I thought I wasn't good enough. But I reckon maybe I am now, thanks to you."

"Don't thank me, Sheriff. You did it yourself," Ned said. He finished his cup and set it down, then looked at the others. "Well, gentlemen, we've got a long way to ride and a disagreeable bunch to take with us. What do you say we get under way?"

"I'm ready," Beck said.

"Aye, me, too," McKirk added, standing up. The three U.S. marshals and the Arkansas sheriff left the restaurant and started across the street to the jail to pick up their prisoners. None of them noticed the man who was watching them from just behind the corner of the livery stable.

Chapter Fifteen

Poke Cates sat on his horse on a low hill just west of Jasper. Poke, Brewster, Athens, Jack Kimmons, and Curly had spent the night camped just out of town. Early this morning Poke had ridden into town to have a look around. Poke was chosen to go into town because he was the only one that Marshal Remington and his deputy, McKirk, hadn't seen when the two lawmen visited the Kimmons place near Tahlequah.

"Well?" Jack asked.

"It's just like we figured," Poke said. "The sheriff's got all four of them boys locked up now, an' the word is that Remington's gonna move 'em back up to Missouri to be hung."

"Damned if I'm gonna let that son of a bitch take my brother up to Missouri," Jack swore.

"When are they plannin' on leavin'?" Athens wanted to know.

"This mornin', I reckon. I heard the liveryman tell the colored boy he's got workin' for 'im to get the horses ready."

"D'ya get us any grub to take along?" Athens asked.

"Yeah, got this," Poke said. He pulled a piece of oilcloth from his saddlebag and unwrapped it. Inside the bundle were a large chunk of well-cooked beef and a slab of uncooked bacon. "Got a loaf o' Indian bread too," Poke added. "It's in the other saddlebag."

"Let's eat a little breakfast now, then trail 'em outta here," Athens suggested. "When the time's right, we'll make our move."

Athens began carving pieces of meat off the big chunk while Brewster cut slices off the loaf of bread.

"Who'da thought that marshal coulda rounded all of 'em up?" Curly asked, wrapping a slice of bread around a piece of the meat.

"They had to trick 'em, or get 'em one at a time," Jack insisted. "Hell, look at what happened to me back to Tahlequah. I woulda taken that marshal on iffen he hadn't had the Scotsman backin' his play. Even then I mighta done it if I'd knowed there weren't no one else with the drop on me."

No one believed Jack, but no one wanted to challenge his statement, so they let it pass.

Athens raised his canteen and chased the last of his breakfast down his throat with the sweet spring water they had filled their canteens with last night.

"Reckon we better get started," he said. "Guess we'll pass around Jasper, just so's no . . . good citizen"—he screwed up his mouth to say "good citizen"—"takes a notion to ride out an' warn the marshal we're comin'."

"Let's get goin', then," Jack said, climbing on his horse. "I wanna get my brother away from them bastards."

It was sunny that same afternoon in Galena when Judge Barnstall walked down the stairs from his office and into the barbershop.

"Good afternoon, Judge," Fred Loomis said, smiling broadly at the jurist when he stepped inside. Though the barbershop was mandated for the prisoners, the judge, his special police force, many of the lawyers, and all the clerks of the court also used it. As a result it had taken on all the appearances of a regular barbershop, complete with mirrors and shelves filled with sweet-smelling, brightly colored tonics and lotions. A large clock hung from one wall, the numbers marked on the face in Roman numerals. The clock hadn't been there during Binder's term. It was Barnstall's idea; he wanted the prisoners to be reminded that their life was now measured in hours and its sweetness was no longer theirs to enjoy as a result of their criminal actions.

"Afternoon, Fred," Barnstall returned. Fred whipped the cover away and Barnstall sat in his barber chair. "Pretty day today," he added. "I may take a walk around town after my haircut. I don't have another case until four this afternoon, and I don't want to stay in the office."

"Oh yes, sir, it's quite a lovely day today," Fred agreed. "A little off the top, as usual?"

"That'll be fine."

"I've got a fresh bottle of rose tonic," Fred offered. "Would you like me to use it on you?"

Barnstall chuckled. "Fred, when the prisoners

come before me I want them to smell sulphur, not roses."

Fred laughed, a high-pitched, nervous laugh. "You want them to smell sulphur, not roses. That's very good, Judge," he said nervously. He was always nervous around the judge... not that he was afraid for his own safety, just that he found proximity to a man with the power of life and death to be intimidating.

Fred had begun working on the judge's hair when the door opened and Jim Early stepped inside. Early had a big smile on his face.

"News?" Barnstall asked.

"All of 'em," Early said. "We just got a wire from Jasper. Ned and the others are bringin' back all four of the men they went after."

Barnstall slapped his hand against the arm of the chair. "Now, by God," he said, "now I can rest at night, knowing that justice is about to be served. Does anyone else know?"

"Not yet. The wire just arrived two minutes ago. I came to you first."

"Good, good," Barnstall said. "I want to tell Jedediah myself. Then you can go down to the newspaper office. I want the whole town to know it."

As soon as Barnstall finished with his haircut, he sent for Jedediah, asking the boy to come up to his office. A few moments later he heard the boy arriving, running up the steps in youthful exuberance.

"You sent for me, Cousin Sam?" the boy asked, pushing through the door without bothering to knock.

"Yes, my boy, I did," Barnstall said. "I just received news that Marshal Remington and his deputies have caught the four outlaws they went after. I expect they'll be back in a few days. I thought you might want to know."

"Yes, sir," the boy said. Barnstall was pleased to notice that the expression on Jedediah's face was just as it should be... not fiendish joy, not youthful bravado, not fear. It was an expression of determination. "Now it's like you said, ain't it, Cousin?" Jedediah said.

"What do you mean?"

"Every man has to do his job. Marshal Remington and Deputies Beck and McKirk done theirs; it's up to me to do mine."

"I reckon it is at that, Jedediah," Barnstall said gently. He reached out and put his hand on the boy's shoulder. "Are you up to it?"

"Yes, sir. When it comes time for me to testify, I'll say just exactly what I saw."

"That's all we want," Barnstall said. "I have to warn you, though, the prosecutor will try and confuse you. He'll try and make you think that you made a mistake when you picked out their pictures. He'll try and make you change your story."

"I didn't make no mistake," Jedediah said. "I seen 'em do what they done to my ma and sister; then I seen 'em kill my pa. I ain't gonna change my story."

"Good boy," Barnstall said, squeezing the boy's shoulder affectionately.

Barnstall watched the boy leave his office, walking higher and straighter than he had ever seen him before. The boy had been living with him ever since he came to Galena, and he was going to live with him until after the trial. After the case was closed, Jedediah would go to St. Louis, where he would live with his mother's sister and her husband. Because it was the boy's mother's branch of the family, they weren't even a part of Barnstall's kin, so he didn't know when, or if, he would ever see the boy again. There was a part of him that wanted to just keep Jedediah here in Galena. He had grown close to him ... had enjoyed the boy's company, and the responsibility for him. But Jedediah's aunt Louise was anxious to get him, had already written half a dozen letters telling the judge about the advantages of the wonderful school Jedediah would be attending, about the room that had been prepared in their house for him, about the clothes and things they had bought for him. Barnstall knew that the couple had been childless and the opportunity to take Jedediah into their home had been a godsend. He knew they would provide the boy with everything he needed, not only the creature comforts but the gentle touch of a mother's love as well.

Barnstall could provide none of that for him. And, with the fullness of his docket, he couldn't even provide the time Jedediah would need. Besides that, Barnstall knew that if the boy were raised in the shadow of the gallows, he couldn't help but feel the effect of it in his own life. Therefore, though Barnstall had enjoyed the temporary condition of surrogate fatherhood, he realized that it could only be temporary.

The newspaper carried the story that afternoon, giving the column feature position on the page.

OUTLAWS CAPTURED

Marshal Remington,
Deputies Beck and McKirk

Do their Duty

Will appear before Judge Barnstall

The paper was taped up to the front window of the newspaper office and sold on the street corners and in the taverns and restaurants of the town. When Jim Early went into one of the local taverns after duty that night, he saw the paper tacked up on the wall.

"Hello, Marshal Early!" the bartender called happily. The bartender drew a beer and set it in front of Early. "This here'n's on the house," he said.

"What for?" Jim asked.

"What for? Why, man, to celebrate," the bartender replied. "What for do you think?"

"Don't think I don't appreciate a free beer," Jim said. "'Cause I do." He picked the beer up and blew some of the foam away. "And I intend to appreciate this one. But I didn't have nothin' to do with capturin' these outlaws. That was all Ned's doin'. Ned, Tom Beck, and John Angus McKirk."

"Sure, I know that," the bartender said. "And I intend to give 'em their free beer soon as they get here. But you the only one I can reward right now. Look," he said, taking in the crowded tavern with a sweep of his hand. "Look at all the business the news has brought me tonight. Ever'where you go you hear people talkin' about it, an' they're all sayin' the same thing."

"What are they saying?"

"Last week, when the judge hung three at the same time, why, we got took notice of as far away as St. Louis. Think what's gonna happen when the judge hangs four! Once news of this gets out there'll be people comin' from hunnerts of miles away, just to be a eyewitness to history. An' the more people that comes to Galena, the more business we're gonna do. Not just me . . . all the businesses, all over town. That's what's got ever'one so excited."

"I see," Jim said. "What if the judge doesn't sentence them all to hang?"

"Are you kiddin'? He is, ain't he? I mean, look here, you don't think there's no chance he won't sentence 'em all, do you?"

"I don't know. That's a decision only the judge can make."

"They're guilty as sin, ain't they? Ever'body says the boy picked 'em out of some wanted posters, an' the neighbors seen 'em hangin' aroun' that day. The judge has got to hang 'em all."

"You're anxious to see justice served, are you?" Jim finished his glass and put it down on the bar.

"What? Oh yeah, justice. Well, yeah, that, too. But the most important thing is to get all four of 'em hung on the same day. Can you imagine the folks that'll come to see that? Want another beer?"

"No, thanks," Jim said. "I've got to be goin'."

Jim left the tavern and walked through the town. The night air was soft and pleasant, neither too warm nor too cold. It was the kind of night you would want for a street dance, a picnic, or an outdoor church meeting. But those were all tame pursuits, and the attitude of this town right now was anything but tame.

Jim heard a commotion from near the gallows, and he walked over to see what was going on. There were a couple of dozen people standing around looking at a large, hand-lettered sign that stood in front of the gallows.

> ON THIS GALLOWS, OUR OWN
> EXECUTIONER WILL HANG
> JACOB NEWSOME
> EPHRAIM FLATT
> THOMAS GERNER
> AND
> WILLIAM KIMMONS.
> THESE FOUR MURDERERS
> WILL BE SENTENCED BY
> JUDGE SAMUEL PARKHURST BARNSTALL
> AND LEGALLY SENT
> TO MEET THEIR MAKER.
> ADMISSION IS FREE.

Jim crossed the square, then climbed the steps to Judge Barnstall's office. He knocked and was invited in.

"Did you see the sign down by the gallows?" Jim asked.

"What sign?"

Jim told him, and Barnstall walked over to the window and looked down toward it. He couldn't read it, but he did see the crowd. He chuckled.

"You don't approve of it, do you, Judge?"

"I can't really say I don't approve, Marshal," Barnstall said. "Whoever painted the sign told the truth, pure and simple. But I reckon it might give the appearance of not giving the scum due process, so you better take it down." He poured a brandy for each of them. "What do you say we drink a toast to Ned, Tom, and John Angus?"

"To three iron men," Jim replied.

Chapter Sixteen

Ned rode with his two deputies and the four prisoners back toward Missouri. Tom Beck was leading the party, and Ned noticed that his deputy kept shifting positions in his saddle in an attempt to ease the pain in his hip. Ned could understand Beck's discomfort, for he was having to do the same thing to keep his side from hurting. McKirk was favoring an arm.

"How are you doing, Tom?" Ned called ahead.

"I wouldn't want to break a bronco about now," Tom answered.

"Nae, nor would I be for fallin' a winter's firewood," McKirk offered. "What about ye, laddie? How's the side?"

"I'd just as soon not wrestle the county champion, thank you," Ned replied.

"S'posin' you fellas stop an' rest a mite. Me an' the boys could go on ahead," Newsome suggested.

He chuckled. "Then, when you'ns get all rested, why, you could catch up with us."

"Dinna be gettin' any ideas aboot thot," McKirk said. "If we get thot tired thot we need to take a rest, we'll jus' shoot ye an' be done with it."

"Yeah, you crazy Scot, you'd prob'ly do it too," Newsome muttered.

Ned chuckled. "Damn right he would."

"Well, just keep him away from me, that's all I got to say."

"Then keep yer mouth shut," McKirk said.

The riders went on in silence for another couple of hours while the miles flowed steadily behind them. Beck, always the wily one, set a pace that would cover ground quickly while sparing the horses as much as possible. They were being very careful with their mounts because it had been a long, hard ride for the animals and they had at least two more days to go before the horses could get a decent rest. Beck took one of the freight roads north that crossed the small creeks but avoided the winding, swift-flowing White River as it snaked toward the mighty Arkansas to the south.

As always in these quiet, reflective moments, Ned contemplated this wild country they were riding through. What most intrigued him were the Ozarks' rivers and streams. Though the mountain waters had been here since the beginning of time, they were never the same any two times he saw them. There were always subtle changes being made in their courses, a carving alteration of the banks, a carrying away of trees and shrubs. Islands were born in mid-channel this year, only to disappear next; flowers would bloom overnight, creating vivid splashes of color.

The rivers were especially different from season to season. In the spring there would be the big floods with their flat tan color and the audible hiss of sand being borne along to sweep out the debris left by ice and snow from the previous winter. In the summer the water was its bluest, but in the fall the rivers would become their most colorful, reflecting from their surface the leaves of gold, orange, russet, red, and brown.

Ned could always go to the woods or mountains and find for himself a comfortable place in the order of things. In the early days, after his wife was killed and Katy suffered her spells, Ned could ride through the hills and realize moments of revelation when man and nature made gut-level sense. All means by which man measured his success or failure became insignificant in a world that fit together as completely as the nature of these mountains.

Though Ned had taken Katy to a convent for her convalescence, he did not consider himself a religious man. Nevertheless, when he came to the woods under such circumstances, he could never help but thank the Great Spirit that he was allowed to be a part of such an existence that included places like these mountains, forests, rivers, and streams.

Gradually the eastern horizon in front of them began to darken while in the west the sun blazed golden red as it settled behind the hills. Ned turned and saw the glow on a puff of dust hanging in the air about three miles behind them. Earlier in the day he had seen a flitting shadow in the woods, and though he had passed it off as a deer, he now began having second thoughts. He said nothing to the others.

The land was a continuous roll of hills, like giant waves on a storm-tossed sea. There were gentle climbs and steep bluffs, wide valleys and sharp gullies. And from here for as far as he could see, the land was just the same.

They camped the first night alongside a wide, swift, shallow stream off the Harrison freight road. The spring was more difficult to cross than it looked because the water was ice cold and swiftly moving, the rocks slippery. They camped on the opposite bank, but no one made any motion to start a fire.

"Hey," Gerner complained. "What about a fire? You got to feed us, give us coffee, keep us warm. That's your duty."

"The only duty we have is to get you back for your hangin'," Ned said.

Beck pulled out strips of dried beef, handed a piece to each of the prisoners, then sat down and started gnawing on a piece of his own.

"I reckon you seen it too, didn't you?" he said.

"Riders in the woods, a puff of dust on the trail behind us? Yeah, I saw it," Ned said.

"Who you think they may be?"

Ned spread out his bedroll and lay down. "Could be Jack Kimmons and the bunch we ran into back at Tahlequah," he suggested.

"Aye," McKirk added. McKirk had just relieved himself against a nearby tree and was buttoning his trousers as he came back to join the others. "I been seein' 'em too, an' there's nae doubt in my mind thot's who 'tis."

Bill Kimmons snickered. "Well, now, reckon there won't be no sleep for you fellas tonight, will there?" He lay back and folded his hands behind his head. "How 'bout that, boys? We'll be restin' all comfortable while they're gonna have to stay awake an' on the lookout."

"It won't do them no good to stay awake," Gerner said. "I know them boys. They can move through these woods quiet as smoke. Why, they'll be in here cuttin' your throats afore you know what's happenin'." Gerner made a raking sound with his mouth and moved his hand across his neck in the symbol of a knife. All the prisoners laughed.

"Shut up," Beck said.

"What's the matter, Deputy? Do you find it troublesome to think about gettin' your throat cut?"

"If ary a throat gets cut tonight, mister, it's gonna be yourn," Beck said menacingly.

"Dinna let 'em get yer goat, laddie," McKirk said to Beck. "They dinna know what they're talkin' aboot."

"No, but they are right about one thing," Ned put in. "We can't all go to sleep. One of us is going to have to be awake all the time. Tom, how 'bout you take from now to midnight, John Angus from midnight till about four, an' I'll take from four till dawn."

"All right," Beck agreed.

Ned and McKirk spread out their own bedrolls and lay down to listen to the dark orchestras of crickets, the monotonous thrum of frogs in bass counterpoint. The prisoners continued to talk, trying to taunt the men. Their taunts began to fade in fervor against the marshals' deliberate wall of silence. Then Newsome tried a new tactic.

"Hey, Bill, you remember that little ol' girl we had our way with? How old was she, did you make it? 'Bout twelve, thirteen, maybe?"

"Naw, she were older'n that. She was tittied up purt' good, iffen you recall. She were fourteen, maybe fifteen."

"Them purt' little ol' tits don't mean nothin'. Hell, I seen lots o' girls gets tits at twelve, eleven even. This girl weren't no more'n twelve. Oh, but she was fine, warn't she?"

"Iffen you was to ask me, I liked the mama the best," Flatt said. "I don't like them little ol' girls with little bitty tits. Now the mama... she was round 'n' soft, and knowed what it was like to have a man ridin' 'er."

"You know what I liked?" Gerner added. "I liked lookin' into Parkhurst's eyes whilst you fellas was puttin' the boots to his wife and girl. Then, when we cut his throat with that there knife, why, he just—"

That was as far as Gerner got, because Beck kicked him in the face, knocking loose a handful of teeth.

"Hey, what the hell? You gone crazy?" Newsome shouted. Beck leaped on Newsome then and started pounding him in the face with his fists.

"John Angus! Get him off!" Ned said. "Pull him off before he kills one of them."

"Kill them? By God, I'm going to cut their livers out an' feed raw meat to 'em as they're dyin'!" Beck swore. He jumped from Newsome to Kimmons and punched Kimmons in the nose. Kimmons's nose had been broken by Ned in the fight the night before, and he let out a bellow of pain when Beck hit him there again.

"Here, easy, laddie, easy," McKirk said, moving quickly to pull Beck away from them. "Would ye be cheatin' the hangman out of his show, now?"

"Did you hear them, John Angus? Did you hear what they was talkin' about?"

"Aye, laddie, I heard, an' it'll be those same words I'll be speakin' before His Honor's court too.

They stand convicted by their own foul tongues, don't ye see?"

"They better watch what they say from now on or I'll be on them ag'in," Tom said.

"Yes," Ned said. "And you'll be doing what they want you to do. They're tryin' to get you to lose your temper so you lose control. Now come on, Tom, you been around long enough to know better'n that."

Beck was panting heavily, looking at the three men he had attacked. Gerner was conscious but still spitting teeth. Newsome's ear was bleeding, and he was complaining that Beck had nearly torn it off. Kimmons was holding his nose and moaning quietly. Only Flatt had escaped Tom's wrath.

"Don't let that crazy man around me," Flatt pleaded.

"If you don't want him on you, I advise you to keep your mouth shut," Ned said.

"Aye," McKirk added. "Could be that the next time I'll be helpin' the mon 'stead of pullin' him off."

About an hour after that, Ned, who had been sleeping, was awakened by a rifle shot. He sat up quickly.

"It's all right, Marshal," Beck said quietly. "Our company's just shooting in the woods to make us nervous. They don't have any idea where we are."

"We're over here!" Newsome shouted.

Ned cocked his pistol, and the sound of the cylinder turning could be heard very clearly. The click of the gear locking into place froze the prisoners into silence.

"You call out again and you're a dead man," Ned said quietly.

McKirk got up and stretched. "'Tis aboot time I took my turn, I'm thinkin'."

"You got another hour if you want," Beck offered.

"Nae. 'Twould do no good to try an' go back to sleep now; this disagreeable mon saw to thot."

"Woke you up, did I? Well, what a shame," Newsome taunted.

"You'll nae mind if I take a pee before I start my watch?" McKirk asked. He walked over to stand above Newsome, then began relieving himself on the prisoner.

"Hey! Hey, what the hell are you doin'?" Newsome shouted, spitting and coughing.

"Oh, woke you up, did I? Well, now, what a shame," McKirk said.

Ned and Beck both laughed.

"If the rest of ye gentlemen are listenin'," McKirk said, "I want ye to know I intend to kick the teeth out of the next mouth that calls out. An', Flatt, for ye I'll be chargin' a dentist's fee besides, for it'll be an improvement to that ugly mug of yours."

There was some quiet grumbling from the prisoners, but it was soon evident that none of them wanted to try the Scot's patience any further.

"Ned. Laddie, 'tis your time," McKirk said, gently shaking Ned.

Ned sat up and stretched, then looked toward the prisoners.

"Sleepin' like babies they are," McKirk said.

"Heard anything from our tagalongs?"

"Nae a sound. I think they'll be waitin' till light before they try their next move."

"You're probably right," Ned said. "All right, Scottie, try an' get some rest."

"Aye. Laddie, I tell ye, I'll be sleepin' a week when we get back, an' woe to the man or woman who wakes me."

Ned smiled. That was as close as McKirk had ever come to saying that there was a woman living out in his cabin with him.

Ned walked over and found a seat on a tree stump, then looked out into the forest. He saw the soft glow of swampfire, listened to the thrum of bullfrogs, the calls of whippoorwills. Behind him he heard the snores and measured breathing of the other men, and he wished he could return to his own bedroll and go back to sleep.

McKirk was right . . . this trip was turning into one long period of exhaustion. Whoever was out there waiting for them had to know that, and they had to know that exhaustion was their ally. Most likely they would make their move tomorrow night.

Ned got up and walked over to his saddlebag. He took out a piece of dried beef, then returned to the tree stump and began chewing on it. He wasn't hungry, but eating would help wake him up. Once he was wide awake he would have no trouble staying that way.

Ned thought about the next night. Tired as they all were now, it would be worse then. They wouldn't be at their best tomorrow night. All right, then, he declared. They wouldn't wait until tomorrow night. He would make something happen during the day. He wasn't sure what it would be, but he would figure something out.

McKirk was asleep now and began to snore loudly, and Ned thought about him peeing on Newsome, then chuckled. McKirk was not a man you got on the wrong side of. A lot of men never learned that until it was too late.

Chapter Seventeen

It was too dark to trail the marshals any farther, so Athens told the others they would have to find a place to camp. They decided to camp on the high ground so they could look around tomorrow before they left, to see if they could spot Remington and the others. They left the trail and started loping up a nearby hill when they happened onto a little house looming blackly in the dark.

"Hey, Athens, do you see what I see?" Brewster asked in a hoarse whisper.

"Yeah," Athens answered. He sniffed. "Smells like we're just in time for supper too. Come on, boys, let's go visitin'."

They rode up to investigate, their horses moving quietly and blowing steamy spools of fog in the chill night air. Finding the house seemed to be a stroke of particularly good luck. Marshal Remington and his deputies were out in the chill night air, while Athens,

Brewster, Jack, Curly, and Poke would be spending the night in a warm house. That would make the marshals even more tired and less alert. When it came time to hit them, the advantage would be with the attackers.

Quietly, the five men approached the cabin. Then, with guns drawn, they kicked the door open and burst in.

There were three people in the little cabin: a man, his wife, and their daughter, a girl of about seventeen. They were sitting around the supper table, but the man got up and started for the fireplace, reaching for a rifle that hung from pegs over the mantel.

Jack cocked his pistol and pointed it at the old man.

"Sit down, Pops," Jack said.

"Oh, Eb!" the woman cried. "Do what they say!"

The daughter said nothing. She just looked at the men through big, frightened brown eyes.

Poke walked over to the table and grabbed a piece of meat from the platter. "This looks good," he said.

"What is this?" Eb demanded angrily. "Who are you? What do you want?"

"Who we are don't make no never-mind," Athens said, tearing into the meat. "We need us somethin' to eat an' a place to stay the night."

"You...you're welcome to the food," Eb said. "An' you can stay in the lean-to out back. It's got straw an' a roof 'case it rains."

"We plan to stay in the house," Athens said.

"Papa, they can't stay in the house," the girl said. "Where would they sleep?"

"Haw! Well, now, Brewster, the girl wants to know where at we'll sleep," Curly said. He grabbed himself, rubbing his crotch. "Here I was thinkin' it was gonna be a long, cold, lonely time up here tonight. 'Pears I was wrong about that. I reckon these two ladies will keep us warm."

"Le's see what they got," Poke said. He grabbed the girl's mother and ripped her dress down the front, exposing her breasts. Jack did the same thing to the girl.

"Get away from them!" Eb shouted. He picked up the meat knife from the table and started after one of them, but Athens clubbed him over the head with the butt of his pistol and Eb went down, knocked cold.

"Tie 'im up, gag 'im, and put 'im in the corner," Athens said. He looked at the two women, who were now trying, unsuccessfully, to cover themselves. Athens grinned evilly. "Now, you two'ns is gonna do what we want. Iffen you don't, we'll kill your man."

"Please, don't kill him," the woman begged.

"You gonna be good to us?" Athens asked. "Real good?"

The woman nodded her head as tears slid down her cheeks.

"What about you, girlie? I ain't heard nothin' from you."

"She'll do what you say," the mother promised.

"I want to hear it from the girl."

"Rose, for God's sake, girl, if you want your pap to live, do what they say."

"Is it gonna hurt, Mama?" Rose asked in a weak, frightened voice.

"It won't be more than you can bear, chile," the mother said gently.

"All right, I'll do it," the girl sobbed.

* * *

The cold rain began before dawn and continued to slash down on the small, weather-beaten cabin perched precariously on the edge of a deep hollow. The back door of the house opened, then slammed shut, and Jack Kimmons hurried through the dark and the rain to check on the horses which stood under a lean-to, some thirty yards distant from the main building.

Even the horses would be fresher than the horses Remington and his deputies were riding, Jack thought. He saw their mounts standing patiently, waiting for another day's work. There were no better horses than those raised in the Nations. The Creeks and Choctaws, especially, valued good horseflesh. If they couldn't buy good mounts, they would steal them.

Subconsciously, Jack reached down and felt himself. He was spent and satiated from his times with the woman and her daughter. Both had lain absolutely still, accepting without protest his shoving, grunting, and slobbering over them last night. The woman and the girl had been the same with the others, making no effort to fight them off as, one after another, the men took their turns with the two hapless victims.

Jack told himself it wasn't really rape. They didn't have to beat the woman into submission... all they had to do was threaten to kill the old man. To save his life, the women allowed Jack and the others to have their way with them, to do whatever they wanted to do. The only sounds the women made during the whole night were their pitiful entreaties to spare the old man.

The old man said nothing at all. He couldn't

speak, because he was tied and gagged and left in the corner to watch while Jack and the others used his wife and daughter.

They forced the women to fix breakfast for them, and when Jack returned to the kitchen it was filled with the rich aroma of coffee. Athens was leaning against the sideboard drinking a cup while he watched the two women. The mother and daughter looked haggard and drawn as they worked. Neither had been able to get a wink of sleep last night and, though neither had been beaten, they both looked as if they had been whipped. The old man was still sitting in the corner, still bound and gagged, looking on with eyes that were alternately filled with hate for the invaders of his home, compassion for his wife and daughter, and shame for being unable to protect them from such a thing.

"D'ya check the horses?" Athens asked.

"Yes," Jack said. "They're fine."

The girl opened the oven and tried to remove a pan of biscuits, but she was so frightened she forgot to use a pot holder. She burned her hand and dropped the biscuits on the table with a shout of pain.

"Girl, don't you know a biscuit pan is hot whenever it comes outen the oven?" Poke asked.

"It warn't hot, Poke. It just didn't take her long to look at it," Brewster said, then laughed at his own joke.

"Iffen you want some eggs I'll have to go out to the nest," the woman said. "See what we got."

"Yeah, eggs would be good," Curly said.

"We ain't got time," Athens said. He grabbed a biscuit, broke it open, and laid a couple of pieces of bacon on the steaming bread. "Jus' make yerself a couple o' bacon an' biscuits, then we'll be on our way."

"You're leavin', then?" the girl asked.

"I know it's gonna break your heart to see me go," Jack teased. "But we got some business to tend to."

All the men scooped up the biscuits and bacon, then trooped out to their horses. They started to mount up; then Athens stopped.

"What is it?" Jack asked.

"You know we can't leave the old man," he said. "He knows this country better'n we do—he could get that long gun o' hisn an' lay up some'eres and pick us off one by one."

"Yeah," Jack said. "You're right."

"Which one of you wanna take care of it?"

"I'll do it," Jack said.

Jack went back to the house and pushed the door open. The two women had already taken the ropes off Eb, and he was starting toward his rifle. Jack smiled.

"I reckon Athens was right."

"No!" the woman screamed as she saw Jack raise his pistol. Jack shot the man just as he reached his rifle. He laughed as the woman and her daughter ran, crying, toward the slumped figure.

"Come on!" Athens called. "It's light... they'll be on their way by now!"

Under the cluster of trees where they had spent the night, Ned and his group mounted up for the day's ride. They were wet, and cold, and tired, but they had one more full day and night ahead of them. They were all wearing oil slickers and wide-brimmed hats to keep out the rain. The road they had planned to follow was covered with water and flushed with mud, so that it wasn't much easier than the forest trails they had been on the day before.

McKirk stood in his stirrups, scratched his crotch, then settled back again. He looked toward Ned. "D'ya hear that shot a while back?" He squirted a stream of tobacco juice toward a mud puddle, where it swirled brown for a moment, then was quickly washed away.

Ned took off his hat and poured water from the brim, then put it back on to cover his wet hair. He reached down and patted his horse soothingly.

"Yeah, I heard it," he said.

"Warn't no hunter," McKirk said. "That was a pistol shot."

"I know. What I don't know is what they were shooting at. Or why."

"Maybe they got in a argument, one of 'em shot one of the others."

Ned chuckled dryly. "That'd be a good piece of news," he said.

"What'll we do next?" McKirk asked.

"We're not gonna follow the road," Ned said. "We're cuttin' off up at Burlington, headin' for Kirbyville past Murderer's Rocks."

"Sartin ambush there," McKirk pointed out.

"That's why we'll do 'er. Better to have it out than fight shadows."

Beck passed out a strip of dried beef to each prisoner. Gerner, whose mouth was sore and missing several teeth from his encounter with Beck the night before, complained.

"I can't eat this. I ain't got no teeth left for to chew."

"Gum it," Beck said without compassion.

* * *

"They left the road here," Poke called out to the others. "See, they went off thataway." Poke pointed due north. The road, though headed in a general northerly direction, made a slight swing to the east here. It was obvious from the tracks that Remington and his group had gone straight.

"Where you think they be headed goin' that way?"

"That's a puzzle, all right," Poke said. "They be wantin' to get on up to Galena; maybe they be joinin' the road ag'in up ter Omaha."

"Naw. They wouldn't do that," Athens said. "They'd go faster stickin' to the road. They won't want to cross the river twice."

"Could be they're headed for Murderer's Rocks," Jack suggested.

"Murderer's Rocks!" Athens said. He smiled broadly. "Boys, we got 'em right where we want 'em. We can set up a ambush there, pick 'em off one at a time."

"Could be they're plannin' to ambush us," Jack warned.

"Naw. They only got one thing on their minds, an' that's to get their prisoners back to Missouri. Come on, we got us some ridin' to do."

Ned and the others rode on through the gray morning. The pouring rain turned to drizzle; then the drizzle stopped, and by noon the clouds rolled away. The sun beat down on them, and they had to strip out of their slickers because they were beginning to steam. By late afternoon their clothes were completely dry, and by nightfall, as they reached Murderer's Rocks, the stars were shining brightly. It was a soft, clear night.

It was quiet. The first whippoorwill began its threnodic call; then the crickets vied with the bullfrogs for noisiness. A cock owl voiced a throaty hoot.

"Thet ain't no owl," observed Tom Beck.

"Nae."

"Check your loads," Ned said quietly.

In the dark, while they were riding, pistols and rifles were checked for loads.

"I'm ready, Marshal," Beck said.

"Aye, me, too."

"All right, I've got an idea," Ned said.

"It ain't gonna work," Newsome scoffed.

"You better hope it works, Newsome," Ned said. "'Cause if it don't, you're the one whose lamp goes out first."

Ned had Beck and McKirk gag the prisoners. Then they switched horses with the prisoners. After that they got down and walked among them on foot, concealed by the animals. They came under the shadow of the rocks and it grew even darker.

It was quiet. Men and animals moved as softly as drifting smoke.

"That's them," Jack hissed. He and the others were in position on Murderer's Rocks, lying with their weapons pointed in the direction from which the marshals would have to come. They had ridden their animals hard, no longer attempting to track but just counting on their feeling that they were going to the right place. Now it appeared that their hunch was right.

"Hold your fire till they get a little closer," Athens warned.

"Don't nobody shoot Remington," Jack hissed.

"He's mine. I owe him. I reckon after tonight there won't be no more question 'bout him backin' me down."

"Not exactly like callin' him out, though, is it, Jack?" Brewster said.

"After this is over, I'm callin' you out," Jack said.

"If you two don't shut up, this ain't gonna get over," Athens warned. He stared down at the shadows. "Maybe we better call down there . . . see if Bill and the others are all right. Could be some kinda trick."

"What kinda trick?"

"How the hell do I know? I just know I don't trust those bastards, that's all."

"I'll find out," Jack said. He cupped his hand around his mouth. "Bill? Bill, it's me, Jack! We're comin' to get you, Bill! . . . Jake? Jake, are you there? Can you hear us?"

"You got 'em marked?" Ned asked.

"Aye, laddie. I'm ready."

"Me, too," Beck said.

"You better be, 'cause I got a feeling this ball's about to open," Ned said.

Chapter Eighteen

"Hell, I don't see but four men," Jack said. "They's s'posed to be seven. Where are the others?"

"Ride in on 'em!" Athens shouted.

Ned, Tom, and John Angus pulled up their horses, dropped to their knees, and fired. A bushwhacker dropped from the saddle and skidded across hard ground. All hell broke loose as flashes of orange light exploded like fireballs on the rocks.

"It's Remington!" Athens shouted. "They're behind the horses!"

Athens's men scattered, frightened and surprised by the marshals' sudden and unexpected appearance. They tried to return fire, but in the darkness and confusion their aim was ragged. Flying lead whistled through the air, whined off stone, rattled on leaves like hail.

McKirk picked out a rider and with one shot tumbled him from his saddle.

"What the hell? Where are they?" Jack shouted in anger and frustration.

"Ever'body get under cover behind the rocks!" Athens called, pointing toward the boulders they had just come from. The bushwhackers started back, but Ned laid his sights on one and fired. Now there were only two bushwhackers on their feet.

"Son of a bitch! Let's get outta here!" Athens shouted.

"No! I ain't goin'! Remington! Remington, I'm goin' to kill you, you son of a bitch!" Jack shouted. He started walking toward the little group of horses and men, firing his pistol with every step. "Come outta there, you bastard!"

"Here I am, Jack," Ned said calmly, stepping out into the open.

Jack fired at Ned, but he was almost insane with rage and frustration, and his bullet hit the ground between Ned's feet, then whined out over the valley behind him. Ned returned fire, and Jack crumpled with a bullet in his chest.

Athens tried to use the moment when Ned was busy with Jack to get in his own shot. Beck saw him and brought him down at about the same time Jack was hit. The entire episode took less than a minute, and now five men lay on the ground. Jack and Athens were dead; Curly, Poke, and Brewster were groaning in pain.

It was early morning, though the sun was full up and the town was washed in a clean, white light, when Ned and his deputies brought the prisoners in to Galena. As they rode through the street they saw the early risers. There were housewives in their backyards doing the wash, shopkeepers sweeping off their porches, and the blacksmith firing up his forge.

Ned found something reassuring about the town's morning activity, as though it were a promise that the world didn't consist entirely of such creatures as the men they had taken prisoner.

They stopped in front of the courthouse, and Jim Early came down to meet them.

"Have any trouble?" he asked.

"No," Ned answered easily. He ran his hand through his hair, across his chin. "It'll be good to get a bath, shave, haircut, hot breakfast, and about twelve hours of sleep, though."

Jim laughed. "You look like you could use all of it," he said. He looked at the prisoners, sullen and morose. "So, this is the scum you brought back?"

"This is it," Ned said. "Where's the judge?"

"Up in his office," Jim said. "I'll tell him you're here.

"I want you to look out this window, Jedediah," Judge Barnstall was saying. "Tell me if you see anyone you recognize."

Jedediah looked through the window and smiled broadly. "Why, there's Marshal Remington," he said. "When did he get back? I thought—" The boy stopped in midsentence and the smile left his face. "Cousin," he said, pointing with a small but unshaking finger. "That's them. That's the men who did the bad things to Ma and Pa and my sister."

"Are you sure, Jedediah?" Barnstall asked. "I think that's just some trackers Marshal Remington signed on."

"No, you have to tell him, Cousin Sam," Jedediah insisted. "You have to tell him not to sign those men on. Those are bad men. They are the ones who came to our house."

"You're sure enough about it to say so in court?" Barnstall asked.

"Yes, sir."

"Now, boy, this is very important. If you identify these men as the ones who killed your family, I'm going to hang them. So be very sure about what you're saying."

"I'm sure," the boy said. "They're the ones."

Jim Early came into the office at that moment.

"They're here, Judge," he said.

"Yes, I saw them," Barnstall replied. "What's more important, the boy saw them. He'll be testifying in court."

"When will that be?"

"I see no need to waste time," Barnstall said. "About ten this morning, I reckon."

"You want to come down and take a look up close?"

"No," Barnstall said. "I'll save all my thunder for the courtroom. Just lock them up tight, make certain there's no way they can get away."

"I'll do it," Jim said, starting back down the stairs.

"Oh, Jim?"

"Yes, sir?"

"Tell Ned and the boys I said they did a good job. A damn good job."

Jim smiled. "Glad to." He trooped back down the stairs to where Ned and others waited.

"What's the judge's pleasure?" Ned asked.

"He'll arraign them later this morning," Jim said. "Ten o'clock."

Ned ran his hand across his chin. "I reckon I can

get my cleanin' up done by then. I'll put off the sleep till after it's over."

"What about us?" Gerner asked. "We'ns is jus' as tired as you. We'd like to get a little sleep too."

Early laughed. "I reckon you fellas will be gettin' all the sleep you need soon. In fact, I don't reckon you'll ever wake up, except in hell."

An hour and a half later, Ned stood at the convent gate. He was much more presentable now than he had been when he rode into town earlier this morning. He had cleaned up, though he passed up breakfast in order to come out here. Beck and McKirk were eating a huge breakfast, compliments of Barnstall's court.

The nun who opened the gate recognized Ned and smiled sweetly. He was such a frequent visitor that they allowed him free run of the convent. As soon as she opened the door for him, she melted back into the shadows of the grounds to join the other sisters in their morning rituals.

Ned walked across the courtyard to his daughter's room. He pushed the door open quietly, then slipped inside. Katy was sitting in a chair, looking through the window. Her attention was so drawn to something outside that she didn't even look around. He peered over her shoulder and saw that she was watching a pair of cardinals, a bright red male and a pinkish orange female, cavorting about on a flowering dogwood tree.

"That's real pretty, darlin'," he said.

Ned sat down and watched her for a few moments longer. He saw the joy in her eyes as she looked at the birds, and he thought of McKirk's comment about Katy having "a peace that surpasseth all understanding."

"Darlin', I know you won't know what I'm sayin'," he began. "But I just brought in four men to Judge Barnstall. Four men to stand trial for a crime like that done against you and your ma. I know it isn't the same four men, but, somehow, I feel the scales of justice are a little more in balance today."

One of the birds flew up to the windowsill, sat there for a moment, then flew back to the tree. Katy continued to watch with rapt attention.

"Nothin' will ever bring back your ma, and nothin' will ever ease the pain that's still burnin' down in my heart," Ned said. "But ever' time I'm able to right a wrong, I'm able to stand the pain just a little better. I just wish you had somethin'... some way to help you through this awful time."

"Love," Katy said quietly.

"What?" Ned gasped, unable to believe what he heard. "Darlin'... did you... did you say somethin'?" It was almost too much for him to hope for.

Katy continued to look out the window as if nothing had happened. Ned stared at her in silence. Maybe he hadn't really heard it. Maybe it was just something he wanted so much that he thought he had heard it.

"Yes," he finally said. He cleared his throat. "Well, darlin', I have to go now. The judge wants to arraign the prisoners at ten o'clock. That's about half an hour from now." He started toward the door, then looked back toward the window at his daughter. She turned to him, and he looked into her eyes. For the first time since he had brought her here, he thought he could see something... a light, a question, something other than the flat, dull, unexpressive eyes he had looked into every time he came.

"Love . . . you," she said, speaking the words with great effort.

"Oh, my God," Ned barked. He ran to her and put his arms around her, sobbing as he held her tightly in his embrace.

Ned returned to the courthouse at about five minutes before ten. Beck and McKirk were just outside, standing in front of the scaffold. They looked up when Ned came over.

"Did ye see the lassie?" McKirk asked.

"Yes," Ned answered.

"How was she?"

"Fine," Ned replied. He couldn't share what had happened with anyone yet. He hadn't even told Mother Superior. This was something he would hold in his heart for a while longer before he started trying to find out what it meant.

"Here they come," Beck said, noting the prisoners who were being moved from the holding cell to the courtroom. A man mounted the scaffold and began rigging the sandweight to the rope. The four prisoners looked up at him, and then at Ned and his two deputies.

"You reckon we might make a deal with that judge?" asked Kimmons.

"What do you think?" Ned replied.

The four outlaws looked up and saw Barnstall then. His face was a mask, his eyes narrowed to slits.

"He looks like a buzzard," observed Flatt.

"Or a hawk," said Newsome.

"Well, it ain't over yet," Gerner bragged.

McKirk cocked his pistol, put it next to Gerner's temple.

"Step lively, laddies," he burred. "Ye must nae keep a body waitin'."

The trapdoor sprang and the sandbag smashed to the ground.

Four men jumped involuntarily as they headed toward the courtroom.

Epilogue

Barnstall watched the lamplight flicker on the windowpanes of his office. He sipped the brandy, swirled the amber liquid around in the graceful snifter, sighed deeply. It had been a long, weary day, but he was satisfied. Justice had been served once again.

The rap on his door came as no surprise.

"Come on in, Ned," he said, his voice bereft of its timbre now that he was not sitting in judgment on his bench.

Ned Remington strode through the door. For a moment his tall frame blocked out the light from the lamp and Judge Barnstall sat at his cherrywood desk in shadow.

"Judge," he said.

"Have some brandy, Ned."

"I'll have a cigar. The brandy might come back up."

"You did well today. Switcher will swing."

"I don't feel much about it."

"I know," said Barnstall, pushing back in his chair. This was his haven after he left the court. This was where he got all his thoughts back in alignment. This was when he could taste his work, assess it from a comfortable distance. "He wasn't the one, either."

Remington knew what the judge meant. Every time he brought a man in, there was an emptiness in him. There would be until he found the man who had murdered his wife and brought him to the bar of justice. That hollow feeling that wouldn't go away.

"Swticher is bad enough," said Remington, taking a cigar from the judge's humidor. He twirled it in his fingers, sniffed its musky tobacco aroma. He smelled Havana's fields, its warehouses, the fingers of a woman who had rolled the cigar at a long table while a man read stories from a book. He smelled the St. Louis docks, the tang of the air on the banks of the Mississippi, and he smelled the scent of cedarwood and dried apples. "He's scared enough after seeing those other boys walk to the gallows."

"You did a good job there, too, Ned."

"How's little Jedediah?"

"He's not little anymore. Not inside. I think he handled it well. Things have to come full circle."

"What's that?" Ned struck a sulphur match, bit off the tip of the cigar. He lit the tobacco, drew air through the flame.

"He saw justice in action. He saw the men who broke up his life go to perdition. He saw them perpetrate their vile deeds, and he saw them pay for their crimes."

Remington strangled on the smoke, laughed dryly.

"Hell, maybe he'll grow up to be a lawyer," he said.

"Maybe. It's an honorable profession." Barnstall rocked back in his chair, masked his face in chiaroscuro. "So is yours."

"I never thought of it that way."

"Why do you do it, Ned? Why do you risk your life to bring in men who should be shot in their tracks for what they do?"

"The pay is good," he said wryly.

Judge Barnstall laughed. Then he leaned forward, picked up his snifter, drank the rest of the brandy. His eyes remained steady, unwatered.

"I'll draw up warrants in the morning," he said. "You take Early, two others, go back to Tahlequah."

"Tahlequah?"

"I want you to close down that saloon, bring those men in to my court."

"Might take an army to bring those boys in, Judge."

"That's why I'm sending you and Jim."

"All right."

"Burn it down. Burn that goddamned saloon to the ground, Ned. You hear?"

"I hear you."

But first, he would watch Leroy Switcher go to his Maker on the end of a rope. And he would think about Katy and the man who had ruined her, who was still out there somewhere, living on time borrowed, time that would be called in someday and paid back for an eternity when the trapdoor fell and the rope stretched taut, broke his neck six inches above the ground.

The two men sat there for a long time in silence, each within the shroud of his own thoughts.

They didn't need words to express their respect for one another.

The silence said it all.

CHANCE

The Maverick with the Winning Hand

A blazing new series of Western excitement featuring a high-rolling rogue with a thirst for action!

by Clay Tanner

CHANCE   75160-7/$2.50US/$3.50Can
Introducing Chance—a cool-headed, hot-blooded winner—who knows what he wants and how to get it!

CHANCE #2   75161-5/$2.50US/$3.50Can
Riverboat Rampage—From ghostly spirits on the river to a Cajun beauty who's ready and willing to stoke up big trouble, Chance is the man women love and varmints love to hate!

CHANCE #3   75162-3/$2.50US/$3.50Can
Dead Man's Hand—Framed for murder, the gambling man breaks out of jail and in a fast shuffle heads upriver to settle the score.

CHANCE #4   75163-1/$2.50US/$3.50Can
Gambler's Revenge—His riverboat stolen—all nice and legal—Chance had to look for justice outside the courtroom...if he wanted the *Wild Card* back!

Buy these books at your local bookstore or use this coupon for ordering:

Avon Books, Dept BP, Box 767, Rte 2, Dresden, TN 38225
Please send me the book(s) I have checked above. I am enclosing $_____
(please add $1.00 to cover postage and handling for each book ordered to a maximum of three dollars). *Send check or money order*—no cash or C.O.D.'s please. Prices and numbers are subject to change without notice. Please allow six to eight weeks for delivery.

Name _____

Address _____

City _____ State/Zip _____

CHANCE 4/87

KILLSQUAD

by Frank Garrett

WANTED: A world strike force—the last hope of the free world—the ultimate solution to global terrorism!

THE WEAPON: Six desperate and deadly inmates from Death Row led by the invincible Hangman...

THE MISSION: To brutally destroy the terrorist spectre wherever and whenever it may appear...

KILLSQUAD #1 Counter Attack   75151-8/$2.50 US/$2.95 Can
America's most lethal killing machine unleashes its master plan to subdue the terrorquake planned by a maniacal extremist.

#2 Mission Revenge   75152-6/$2.50 US/$2.95 Can
A mad zealot and his army of drug-crazed acolytes are on the march against America...until they face the Killsquad.

#3 Lethal Assault   75153-4/$2.50 US/$3.50 Can
The Fourth Reich is rising again, until the Hangman rounds up his Death Row soldiers for some hard-nosed Nazi-hunting.

#4 The Judas Soldiers   75154-2/$2.50 US/$3.50 Can
A madman seeks to bring America to its knees with mass doses of viral horror, but Killsquad shows up with its own bloody cure.

#5 Blood Beach   75155-0/$2.50 US/$3.50 Can
The Hangman and his Killer crew go halfway around the world to snuff out a Soviet/Cuban alliance seizing control in Africa.

Buy these books at your local bookstore or use this coupon for ordering:

Avon Books, Dept BP, Box 767, Rte 2, Dresden, TN 38225

Please send me the book(s) I have checked above. I am enclosing $_____ (please add $1.00 to cover postage and handling for each book ordered to a maximum of three dollars). Send check or money order—no cash or C.O.D.'s please. Prices and numbers are subject to change without notice. Please allow six to eight weeks for delivery.

Name _____

Address _____

City _____ State/Zip _____

Killsquad 4/87